SPARRING PARTNERS

and other stories

IAN SEARLE

The stories in this collection are all works of fiction and the characters portrayed
the products of the author's imagination. Any resemblance to a real person,

living or dead, is entirely coincidental.

First published in 2018 by CompletelyNovel.com

©Ian Searle 2018

All rights reserved

ISBN 978 1787232587

Printed in the UK by CPi

It is expressly forbidden to make copies of this book or to

transmit in any form and by any means

without the prior permission of the publisher.

CONTENTS

Sparring Partners	5
Claustrophobia	21
Six Hundred Words	29
Buster	39
The Census	52
In Sickness and in Health	60
The Return	78
Visiting Father	86
The Lantern Room	96
The Omen	111
Protecting Grandad	115
First Impressions	123
Inquisition	127
Charlie the clown.	131
Brief Encounter	135
Bless you – a life story	139
Resting	152
Arkwright	156
Temptation	163
The Bucket List	166
The Corporation	171
A part of the main	174

These 22 stories were written over a period of many years. I thought it about time to do something with them instead of leaving them to turn yellow in a desk drawer. They vary enormously in length (and possibly in quality), and some are quite short. If you read 'Six hundred words', you will understand one of the reasons. I firmly believe that a story, like Destiny, tends to shape its own end, and length is determined by the story itself. I hope you enjoy them. I have enjoyed writing them.

IS

2018

Sparring Partners

(First published in Blackwoods Magazine in March, 1978. Reprinted in Short Story International, New York, July,1978)

"Fish again!" said Father Lenotre, sitting down wearily.

"The Sisters do their best, Father; it isn't easy, you know," Father Barthier said.

Lenotre did not answer, trying hard not to be irritated by this smug little priest who was always so charitable. For three years he had shared his life and work with this man who remained steadfastly cheerful in the face of death, disease, privations, the heat, mosquitoes and all the other oppressive facts of life on this isolated mission. It would be a further four years before his mandatory seven-year term of service expired and the cross would be lifted from his shoulders.

Lenotre's lined face, gaunt with years of hardship and yellowed by quinine, looked briefly even sadder than usual.

"Come now, Father," said Barthier, "it's not that bad; indeed, it's really very good fish. Sister Marie is a remarkable cook. We're very fortunate."

He smiled encouragingly and Lenotre looked at him in disbelief, seeing a round, pink face that retained its colour in spite of the fierce tropical sun.

Why, he wondered, must he continue to jolly me along like a sick child who needs to be humoured.? Why can he not for one instant talk to me as an intelligent adult? Why can't he simply say I'm bad-tempered and should control myself?

But Lenotre said nothing, just ate a little food, pushed the plate away and lit his pipe.

"We're running very low on medical supplies," he said at length.. "I hope the ship arrives soon."

"I'm sure the Bishop is doing his best," said Barthier.

"I'm sure, too. I only wish he could do better. We have almost no drugs left."

"We must have faith, Father."

"We must have quinine, too."

"It will come."

"Yes, of course it will – eventually. But it's already three weeks late. The first week in November, we were told. Now it's December. Christmas will be on us soon."

"Astonishing how quickly time passes, isn't it?" said Barthier. "The last time the ship called we were preparing for Holy Week."

Barthier finished his meal with a couple of mangoes. Then Sister Marie scurried in with the coffee, put it on the table and left without saying a word or raising her eyes. Lenotre poured two cups and drank his quickly. Gratefully, he left the table and went to his room.

Lying half naked under the mosquito net he sweated gently. His book remained unopened beside him. He heard Barthier's bed creak and the grunts and puffing as he arranged himself on the other side of the thin, bamboo wall. After a few minutes the heavy breathing gave way to loud snores. Lenotre heaved a deep sigh of resignation and opened his book.

Lenotre loved the solitude, the chance to reflect, to meditate on his life as a priest, to pray. If only it were not for the snoring, the two-hour silence after lunch would be perfect. A faint breeze stirred the mosquito net. The square hole that was the window showed palm-fronds and a blue sky beyond. The children from the little school had been sent to lie down for an hour before they began their daily gardening. Cicadas sawed away, making their shrill noise that passed unnoticed until it stopped.

Lenotre began to pray. Forgive me, Lord, for my uncharitable thoughts. I really do try to remember all the good things about Barthier. I know he means well and it is I who am at fault. He has a simple faith, Lord, while I am so often troubled with doubts and so easily led into cynicism. It is not his fault he irritates me, and he always seems so cheerful because he believes we all need cheering up. There are times when I feel very old and tired, when my dearest wish is to be alone, as I am now. It is then Barthier annoys me most because he will not leave me alone; he always reminds me of my duty; he always expects me to put on a cheerful face. He makes me feel inadequate, Lord, and that is a heavy cross to lay on any man. I know this is your way of testing me. Help me pass the test; help me keep my patience; help me to be humble. Now I'm being sorry for myself, too, Lord, I'm a weakling. Help me conquer my weakness; help me to think of others, especially of Barthier, and to help him. We have never been close, in all the time we have spent together here. He must have a strength that I lack. I shall try to admire it more.

Lenotre sat up, mopped his forehead and picked up his book. He could not concentrate and, after a minute or two, put the book down again, got off his bed and padded, barefoot, to the shower. The water was warm but refreshing, and yet five minutes later, as he sat on the veranda in clean clothes. He felt as hot as before. There was no escape from the humidity.

He looked out across the sea and indulged in his favourite disciplinary exercise. He forced himself to look at he view and seek again the pleasure it had first given him, the pleasure any newcomer would find.

In front of the house rough grass swept down to the brow of the hill with its fringe of ragged wild shrubs. On either side bushes framed the picture. The tall bare grey trunks of kapok trees rose sharply above shorter, greener crowns. At the foot of the hill, coconut palms swayed slightly, their fronds glittering. The lagoon was a mixture of deep blues and vivid greens where the coral grew relentlessly upwards and through the surface of the water. The surf broke in a white line over an almost continuous barrier reef. Then there was nothing but sea, blue and unbroken. For a moment Lenotre felt again the splendour of the scene which he saw every day.

Suddenly he stiffened and stared hard at the horizon. Returning to his room he fetched his old binoculars and focused them on a small black mark in the distance.

'Father Barthier! Father!' he called.

His companion appeared on the veranda a few moments later. His round face was still bloated with sleep, like that of a small child.

'What is it?' he asked, running his fingers through his disheveled hair.

'The ship. I think it's coming at last. Take a look.'

Rubbing the sleep from his eyes, Barthier took the glasses and looked out to sea. 'Yes,' he said, 'I said we should have faith.'

Lenotre suppressed his irritation. 'She'll just make it by nightfall. We'd better warn the Sisters. The Bishop will want a good meal – and we'd better get the children ready, too.'

There was much to do. It was a point of honour to have the Mission spick and span when the Bishop made his call. The children were recalled from the gardens to tidy the schoolrooms and dormitories. The two priests set about tidying their own house, while the Sisters worked with some of the children in the little church, filling it with flowers and changing the altar cloth, before they set to work in the kitchen, preparing a meal for their visitor.

This was an occasion in every sense: not only were these visits rare – once or twice a year – but they were welcome in many ways. They allowed the Fathers to make confession and provided the opportunity to obtain advice and guidance on the thousand problems which had arisen. For the children there was the chance to show their skills to an important visitor. A visit also provided an excellent reason for having a traditional feast.

At length the preparations were complete: the Mission was neat and tidy and every doorway was fringed with palm-fronds, the ends of which had been stripped to the centre rib and scarlet hibiscus flowers spiked on the tips. Banana leaves were spread in a broad pathway across the lawn and little parcels of food, wrapped in yet more leaves, lay thickly on the improvised table-cloth which was liberally decorated with hibiscus and frangipani blooms. The children were scrubbed and garlanded, their thick, curly hair almost hidden under leaves and flowers. The four Europeans wore spotless robes.

The whole community lined the beach as the schooner tacked to approach the entrance to the lagoon. She was painted black and stained by the sea; her sails were brown. She was business-like, but to the watchers on shore she was sheer beauty. At length she hove to, her sails were dropped, and the anchor splashed into shallow water. The Bishop was rowed ashore in a dinghy manned by four oarsmen.

He greeted the Fathers and the Sisters in French, then, turning to the children, spoke briefly to them in their own language, saying how pleased he was to see them all again.

He turned back to Father Lenotre. 'Would you ask the children to stay here and help unload the ship while we go on up to the Mission? I'm afraid we must unload tonight and sail again at first light. But I have a surprise for you.'

'A surprise, my lord?'

'Yes, indeed. We have six tea-chests full of gifts from the people of my old parish of Saint Antoine. They made a collection of all kinds of things and sent them to us to give to the Missions – especially with the children in mind.'

At the house the Bishop took a shower before accepting a drink of cold lime juice.

'It's lovely here,' he said, staring out from the veranda as the brief dusk fell. The sky was a blazing mixture of orange and gold; the white line of breakers seemed alive. Lamps on the schooner illuminated it like a chiaroscuro painting. The children, carrying boxes up from the beach, sang as they worked.

Lenotre looked at the Bishop. 'I am sorry you can't stay longer.'

The Bishop turned towards him with a smile. 'And I'm sorry there's so little time to sit and talk. You have a difficult and lonely task to do. The two of you must try to give each other support as well as set an example to your flock. It isn't easy. We will make the most of the few hours we have. First I shall hear your confessions and those of the Sisters; then we shall say a mass.'

Lenotre and Barthier stood on the beach in the early morning and waved a last farewell as the ship sailed away.

'He's a good man,' observed Barthier.

Lenotre could not think of an appropriate answer. He remembered what had passed in the privacy of the confessional and was grateful at least that the Bishop understood his personal trial.

'Yes,' he answered at last, 'I'm always sorry to see him go. He brings a strange comfort with him.'

'Comfort,' repeated Barthier in his most irritating manner. 'That's a peculiar word to use. He is a godly man, of course. Is that what you mean?'

'Yes,' said Lenotre. 'Shall we go back?'

'Let's give the children a treat,' said Barthier. 'They can help to unpack the tea-chests. They'll enjoy that.'

They set out the chests in a line in front of the house. 'Come on, Benedict,' said Barthier to a boy standing near the front of the crowd of curious children, 'You open the first box.'

The boy levered off the lid and began to remove the contents.

'And what have we here?' asked Barthier, in his jolliest voice. Reaching into the chest he pulled out two pairs of boxing gloves. Lenotre could not believe his eyes.

A small boy asked, 'What are they, Father?'

'Boxing gloves, my boy,' said Barthier. He untied them and pulled one on. 'See?'

The children looked at his gloved hand, not understanding.

'They're for boxing; it's a sport,' explained the priest. 'Look.' He put on the other glove, raised his clenched fists in a parody of a prize-fighter and indulged in a little shadow-boxing.

The children were too respectful to laugh, but they were puzzled by the priest's antics.

'I don't think they understand you,' Lenotre observed drily.

'No, I don't think they do.' Barthier was puffing slightly from his exertions. 'Father Lenotre and I will show you,' he said to the children. 'You see, it needs two men. The both wear gloves like these.' He tossed the second pair to Lenotre. 'And they box in a square space – like the veranda there. Come on, Father.' He clambered up the steps and Lenotre followed him.

'Do you think this is a good idea?' asked Lenotre.

'Of course! Is there any better way to explain? Put the gloves on.

Lenotre hesitated, then did so while Barthier tried to explain what boxing was all about.

'You see?' he said. 'The two men shake hands to show they are not real enemies, then they begin to box – to hit each other. Come on, Father!' He threw a playful punch at Lenotre.

Lenotre shrugged. He had become involved in this and did not want to make Barthier look even more foolish in front of the children. He would have to play along with him. He began to spar, flicking lefts at his opponent, who still laughed his jolly laugh and punched playfully back.

Lenotre, tiring of this half-hearted game, stopped moving and dropped his gloves just as Barthier swung a wild right. The blow caught Lenotre square on the left cheek-bone and, for an instant, he saw red. He reacted instinctively and lashed out with a left and a right to the head. The left caught Barthier high up on the temple. A trickle of blood ran down his face. The smile disappeared and on Barthier's face Lenotre was surprised to see an undisguised dislike which matched his own. He wanted to hit that face, to vent the years of frustration on this stupid, pretentious, condescending priest. He did so, lashing out in earnest, forgetful of the surroundings, of the crowd of children watching open-mouthed. Barhier retaliated with less skill but with equal fury, swinging wildly at the taller man, the gaunt, cynical companion who treated him with an almost aristocratic contempt. Fists whirled and smacked, and the two men staggered and gasped on the veranda. Lenotre suddenly unleashed an enormous left hook which knocked Barthier off his feet, hurling him headlong off the veranda to land in a crumpled, senseless heap on the grass.

Lenotre looked down at him, gulping in air and sweating profusely. The children were now terrified, having become aware that the fight was serious. The priest pulled off the gloves and stepped down from the veranda. With the help of several of the children he managed to carry Barthier into the house where they placed him on the sofa. Lenotre told the children to go. They went, quietly and with fearful glances at the unconscious figure on the couch.

There was a large red swelling on Barthier's right cheek-bone. Gently Lenotre pulled the boxing gloves from his companion's hands and fetched a damp face-cloth with which he bathed Barthier's face. A bewildering confusion of thoughts ran through his head. When he hit Barthier he had experienced, momentarily, great satisfaction, but now he felt only shame. Looking down at the still figure he was shocked to find it was like looking at a stranger – the round face, normally full of sincere cheerfulness, was now relaxed into an expression of sadness, almost of suffering. For the first time in three years Lenotre felt real pity and an affinity with the little man.

Barthier stirred and opened his eyes. He looked up at Lenotre and frowned. Gathering himself together, he put a hand up to his face.

'Father,' said Lenotre, 'forgive me. I didn't mean…'

'It's all right,' said Barthier. He tried to smile but winced suddenly at the pain. 'There's no real harm done.'

'Barthier,' insisted Lenotre, 'I think you should know – it wasn't an accident. I wanted to hurt you. I'm ashamed.'

'There's no need,' said Barthier. 'I know you were in earnest. But then, so was I. For a moment we both forgot ourselves. I hope we're both sensible enough to dismiss it from our minds.'

'But I've hurt you!'

'Not seriously. I admit I feel a little shaky, but I expect I'll recover.'

'Let me bring some wine.'

'That would be nice.'

The two men sipped the wine in silence, then Barthier said quietly, 'I had this coming, you know. Perhaps it's as well it happened.'

'What do you mean?'

'I think you know what I mean.' Barthier did not meet his eyes. 'We've lived and worked together for three years in this place; in all that time I've been a great trial to you, I know.'

'A trial?'

'Please, Father, let's be honest with each other. When we joined the Order we both accepted that we had no control over our lives, our place of work, our companions. Personal preferences are not allowed in our work. We promised obedience. It is not always easy. It is probably harder for you than for me.'

Lenotre did not reply. He agreed, although it was a painful truth.

'You see, I'm not a very clever man and I accept it. I just about managed to scrape through all the examinations at the seminary. My only regret is that I can do so little for you because you are intelligent.'

'Even if this were true,' said Lenotre, trying to comfort him, 'there are gifts more important than intelligence – charity, patience, cheerfulness, unselfishness.'

'Perhaps. Perhaps. But for someone like you, Father, I am about the worst companion. I put on a cheerful face every morning, I pretend to be the eternal optimist, to keep everyone cheerful. It's my way of atoning, you see, for my insufficiency. I know you suffer loneliness and the burden of responsibility for the Mission, of caring and planning for the school and the sick. You are so much cleverer than I. You always see the problems first and always find the answers.'

'Oh, come now, Barthier,' said Lenotre, beginning to feel uncomfortable. 'you do your fair share, you know. And you are cheerful. You do a lot of good, putting heart into everybody when the heat gets us down, or when the rains spoil the gardens, or when we're feeling dispirited with fever.'

Barthier shook his head. 'It's only an act, Father. It's all I can do. The trouble is, you know that, and, I regret to say, I resent your knowing it.'

'I don't understand.'

'After three years,' said Barthier, 'I still find you remote. Our backgrounds are so different; your parents were bourgeois, comfortably off, used to mixing with intelligent, well-educated people. I come of peasant stock. I still find it hard to talk to people, so I act a part. I'm the jolly, fat, friendly little priest; you're the clever, sharp and decisive man, destined perhaps for a high post in the Church.'

'You mean I'm cynical and sarcastic.'

'That too, at times, when foolish people exasperate you.'

'Father,' said Lenotre, 'why are you telling me all this? Wouldn't it be better left unsaid?'

'I'm saying it because I need your forgiveness as much as you need mine.'

'My forgiveness?' Lenotre was startled.

'I wanted to knock you down when we started boxing. Inevitably you knocked me out, just as you will always better me at anything. Still, I really wanted to hurt you.'

Lenotre got up and walked towards the veranda. Far out to sea the schooner, a tiny black speck, was about to slide over the horizon. The children had disappeared, leaving a litter of clothing and empty boxes on the grass. Lenotre felt tired and drained, aware of the isolation and the burdens of the work. 'I'm sorry,' he said, with his back to the room. 'You must find me terribly difficult to work with.'

'Not to work with, Father; your work is first class. It's just that we are such an ill-matched pair – me, an inarticulate fool, and you a competent leader.'

'Pride,' said Lenotre, with emphasis, 'that's all it is, dammit. I'm too proud. I keep myself to myself, talk only to the Bishop and to God. I get annoyed with you when you are simply doing what you think is best, instead of treating you with respect as an equal. You are right, Father, to be angry with me.'

'No, you can't justify anger like that.'

Lenotre turned his back on his companion. 'I think you can,' he said, 'because you have taught me a valuable lesson today.'

'What's that?'

'We're both human. I might be a better boxer than you, Father, but I'm certainly not a better Christian. Let's have another glass of this excellent wine, then you can tell me where I can find a hammer and a nail.'

'What do you want them for?'

'You'll see.'

Ceremoniously, Lenotre hammered a nail into the wall. Then he picked up the two pairs of boxing gloves and, tying them together, hung them on the nail. Finally, he poured two glasses of wine. 'A toast,' he announced, 'to the day we discovered we are both human.'

They raised their glasses and drank. Lenotre sat opposite Barthier and smiled at him over his glass.

Barthier lifted his own glass in salute. His pink, round face, still swollen, was completely serious.

Claustrophobia

It was cool and damp in the cave. The three of them picked their way over the uneven floor by the light of torches, too tired to speak. Veronique lit the candle she had left in a crevice of the wall. Bernard and Jean-Jacques shrugged out of their rucksacks and dropped them to the floor. They found empty ammunition cases to sit on, lit cigarettes from the flickering candle flame and wrapped their greatcoats round them tightly in an attempt to fend off the cold.

  Leaning back against the roughness of the cave wall, Jean-Jacques looked at the other two. Veronique was handsome still in a gaunt way. The trials of the past two years had etched themselves into her face. The soft prettiness of the little girl with whom they had attended the village school had disappeared. In its place the set of the jaw and the darkness of the eyes bore witness to a resolve which could never be diverted: she was, he knew, implacable with good cause. She had seen her own daughter destroyed by corrupt soldiers. Raped and then treated by them as an object of ridicule, young Marie had thrown herself off the cliff not half a kilometre from the cave entrance.

  Veronique had shown no sign of grieving as a normal mother would grieve. Instead she had turned in on herself, fierce hatred nursed behind those hard eyes, any indication of feminine softness disappearing under the almost incredible physical energy and stamina on which her hopes of revenge were founded.

She smoked the harsh tobacco and stared at the wall ahead.

Bernard too was smoking nervously. He fidgeted, half turning on his improvised seat to look at the darkness where the entrance was. He tapped his cigarette to knock off the ash at frequent intervals. He was like an animal in a zoo cage. He had always been quick and nervous in his movements. Some people thought it a sign of intelligence. Jean-Jacques saw it rather as a kind of permanent unease, the nervousness of the stammerer, the little boy whose father had beaten him at every opportunity without good reason. Bernard had adopted a wariness which could be very valuable in certain circumstances, when it was dangerous to trust anyone. He moved like a wild deer, ears cocked for the snap of a twig, for the least movement where there should be none.

"Where is he?" he asked.

"Martin? He said he'd be back by 9 o'clock at the latest" Jean-Jacques said.

Bernard looked at his watch. Veronique watched him without moving her head, but Jean-Jacques saw the gleam of the whites of her eyes as they turned.

"It's 8.15 now," said Bernard. He ground out the cigarette on the floor and lit another, the match flaring with a homely noise. "There's no reason he should be that late. It's not that far to St Brieve. He knows the way well enough, God knows."

"He said 9 o'clock, not 8.15."

"I don't like it. He could have run into a patrol."

"Martin isn't a fool. He's on his own because it's safer. He's given himself plenty of time."

"Too much."

Jean-Jacques chose not to answer. Reconnaissance was vitally important. Martin was dependable and careful. He was the explosives expert and he needed to be sure where best to lay the charges tomorrow if the bridge were to blow. According to the intelligence they had by radio, a munitions train was due at about 7 pm: it would be a great coup to get the train at the same time as the bridge, but the bridge, they knew, was well guarded. Martin's report would confirm that it was possible or contradict it. It was worth waiting a few minutes longer to find out.

Veronique leaned back and closed her eyes. If Bernard was a deer, thought Jean-Jacques, she was a lioness: she conserved her energy for the chase, apparently asleep, she was ever alert and ready to spring into action. It was a good analogy: it was the female lions who did most of the hunting and he, the male, the alpha male, relied on Veronique's prowess and ferocity. There were times when he wished he did not have to carry the responsibility for it all.

"I don't like it in here," Bernard said. "I never have. We're rats in a trap. The Bosch only have to seal off the entrance and we're dead."

"They don't know where it is," said Jean-Jacques. "We take plenty of care not to be seen."

Bernard shifted on his seat and shrugged. "I know," he admitted. "It's just that, if they ever did find the place, we'd be absolutely at their mercy."

"But even the entrance isn't really visible!"

Bernard nodded. It was true. It would require very special, local knowledge to find the place. The entrance was narrow, a vertical slit in the rock immediately below a heavy overhang which projected about eight feet. But from the overhang trailing overgrowth hung down in a curtain, obscuring the entrance. It required skill and energy to climb the cliff below, too, and in so doing it was very difficult not to betray your presence by disturbing the loose stones. However, once you were inside the cave itself, and had wriggled your way down the passage, even light was trapped Bernard had always shown signs of claustrophobia, and was eager to escape as soon as possible. When Jean-Jacques had first suggested this as a near perfect hide-out, Bernard had resisted the idea, but even he had to admit it was as safe as anywhere they could think of.

It had been Martin who discovered the cave when they were all children. Martin was the clever one. He and Jean-Jacques had climbed up the cliff one day just to see if there was a ledge behind the hanging creepers. They found the crack in the rock-face and began to explore but it was too dark inside to go far and they returned later. They kept it a secret between them for years. Later they forgot it altogether until one evening when they had been thinking of how best to set up an active Maquis group. The landscape round about was flat and open and although they could get around, particularly at night, without being detected by the occupying Germans, there was nowhere to store supplies, explosives in particular. The cave seemed ideal.

Bernard had a box of matches in his hand and was rattling it nervously. Veronique's eyes snapped open,

"Don't," she said.

Bernard looked at her, surprised.

"I don't like the noise," she said evenly and closed her eyes again.

Bernard put the matches in his pocket and stood up. "I need a pee," he said.

"Stay where you are," said Jean-Jacques. "If you're really desperate, use the other end of the cave."

It was only an excuse to get out into the air again, he knew. Bernard shrugged again, stayed put.

"Eight thirty," he said.

"For God's sake shut up," said Jean-Jacques. "We both know this place makes you nervous, but there's no need to unsettle us as well."

Bernard fell silent.

The candle guttered. Although it was cold inside, Jean-Jacques could see in the light of its flame that Bernard's face was shiny with sweat. It must be like this for people in submarines, only for them the air itself was foetid whereas here at least the air was clean, apart from the smell of dampness. It was never dry, because the water percolated through the rock and here and there produced a sheen like that on Bernard's forehead.

After Jean-Jacques' impatience and Veronique's cold stare, Bernard remained silent for many minutes, but he looked constantly at his watch. After a long time Jean-Jacques looked at his own watch - 8.55, and still no sign of the missing Martin. Bernard's nervousness was growing more obvious by the second.

"I think one of us should go and have a look," he said. "He said before nine o'clock. It's very nearly that now." And he got to his feet.

"Stay where you are!" Jean-Jacques snapped. It was strangely said, almost a hostile command. Bernard looked at him with surprise but did as he was told. Veronique, eyes wide open, remained unmoving. She was no longer in any sense relaxed.

Time passed: nine o'clock showed on the face of Bernard's watch. He stood up again.

"I really think - ," he began, but was unable to finish the sentence. Outside the cave entrance there was a sudden loud explosion and then a terrifying roar as tons of rock began to move. The noise was deafening and from the entrance passage came a cloud of dust which filled the chamber. Bernard cried out in panic and the other two stood up, backs to the wall as the candle went out in the rush of air and debris.

There was a moment of utter blackness and the noise subsided until there was only a faint trickle of small rocks and stones falling outside. Veronique had seized a torch and switched it on. The air was full of dust which danced in the beam of light. The torch picked out Bernard, flat against the wall of the cave, terror on his face.

"Your friends!" said Jean-Jacques.

"I don't know what you mean," he said, held like a frightened rabbit in the beam from the torch.

"They were coming to catch us all," Jean-Jacques said slowly. "Your German friends. We knew, you see. That's why Martin was late."

"No, no," he said. "If the Germans had wanted to seal us off, they would have waited for Martin, too."

"Yes, indeed," said Jean-Jacques. "That's why it was so important to wait until 9 o'clock."

"They would want to capture us, not kill us."

"True."

In the light of the torch's beam, Bernard was bewildered.

"They must have seen Martin and decided to fire at him - maybe it was a mortar."

"They didn't fire at all," said Jean-Jacques.

Bernard licked his lips, at a loss.

"Martin has been waiting outside for them to mount an assault up the cliff. He planted charges under the overhang. He was waiting until the assault party was all on the path directly under it, and then." he clapped his hands together. "We knew, you see."

"But we are as good as dead!" cried Bernard. "Buried alive. We'll all die in here."

"Not all of us," said Veronique. "Just you, you weak, treacherous bastard!"

The hand without the torch held a pistol. In the reflected light it gleamed as she moved her hand. There was a loud bang and Bernard staggered as the first bullet hit him. Veronique shot a further five bullets into his body.

"He was scared," said Jean-Jacques. "Scared of what they would do to his sister."

Veronique said nothing, but calmly put the pistol back in her pocket.

Jean-Jacques stepped past the body and towards the back of the cave. He had a torch in his hand now and he shone it downwards at the very back where the roof of the cave sloped to the floor. He dropped to his stomach and wriggled forwards, thrusting the torch in front of him. There was a very small tunnel which turned sharply to the left before it opened into a second, smaller chamber. Veronique followed him. They crouched under a ceiling which was less than two metres high, but it tapered into a long slit and as they looked upwards, there was a movement and a rope snaked towards them.

"Martin," said Jean-Jacques. "Good man. You go first, Veronique" and he watched as she climbed through the narrow escape hole, agile as a circus acrobat, towards the fresh air of the mountain.

Six Hundred Words

Charles, this is for you to read out to the Creative Writing Group today. I shan't be there. I have not missed a meeting for the past ten years, except when I was ill a couple of times. I don't suppose you remember them. Still, even though I can't attend, I thought I'd leave this article for you and ask you to read it on my behalf.

Six hundred words as usual, that's what you always ask for, no more and no less, so that's what this will be. I'll make sure by getting the word processor to do a word-count from time to time. I'd hate to exceed my allowance.

(114 words so far, by the way.)

I suppose the first question you will be asking is why I'm not at the meeting. I didn't say anything at breakfast and doubtless you are surprised that I haven't turned up. I know you wouldn't wait to begin and I know that you have always insisted on reading out contributions from the absentees first, so this will be one of the first items to be read out. You'll already be taking note of the abbreviations and the non-literary style which makes it sound too colloquial for your taste, and I dare say you are already forming some of your usual judgements, ready to pronounce on my writing ability. Wife or stranger, it cuts no ice with you, as you have said in the past.

(Goodness me! 246 words already! I'd better get to the point pretty quickly before my time is up.)

I would have found it difficult to say any of what I have to say face to face, not because I would be too embarrassed or anything, but simply because I don't honestly think you ever listen to me any more. Whether it is breakfast time or supper, it is always you who seem to have so much to talk about and which you have for years presumed I want to hear. In bed you don't talk at all – indeed, you don't do anything else, either. When I actively consider it, I realise you have never in your life been able truly to listen to anyone, nor have you ever listened to me, either, not really *listened*. Oh, you may have pretended to listen, but, in reality, you were only listening so that you could find counter-arguments to what I said. You always have to have the last word (and you even ration the number of words I can use - 425 now.)

Well, this little literary exercise just might make you stop and reconsider your own limitations. You *have* limitations, you know, although you don't seem to recognise them, and you are never unsure of yourself. I shall say what I have to say in as direct a manner as I can, "a desirable quality in prose," you always say, don't you? I shall keep the paragraphs short, too.

(495 words)

I'm leaving you. I've had enough after fifteen years of so-called marriage. It has *not* been fun. You are a bully and a bore.

You have treated me just as you treat your Creative Writing Group members, indulging them, telling them so patronisingly that they have interesting things to say and then suggesting how they could say them better your way, not theirs. You have spent fifteen years of my life telling me I have a lot to offer you, the family and the world, and then suggesting how I should use these mismanaged talents.

What does the Group really think?

Goodbye,

Caroline.

(599 words. I'll leave you the last one as always, of course.)

Digging up the past.

It wasn't unusual to recruit mature students to help on the dig. David was quite glad of the fact. Enthusiasm was always welcome, but at times the sheer boisterousness of the helpers, especially in the evenings when the day's work was done, could be wearing for someone of his age. On this particular afternoon, David, sitting back on his heels in the trench to ease his back for a moment, could see over the rim the second trench about fifty yards away, his colleague, Moira. She was standing with her back to him, pointing out the work in front of her to a new recruit, a woman of mature build. Good, thought David, we could do with one or two more helpers while this good weather holds. Then he resumed his work.

He was scraping soil methodically from the bottom of the trench. Behind him three other workers worked assiduously and in silence, two young girls, and a young male student, keen to learn, concentrating.

David's trowel revealed a small area of different texture. Automatically he switched to a paint-brush to clear the film of soil. It looked like a shard of pottery. He picked up a knife and began very slowly to pick crumbs of soil away from the exposed artefact. It extended several centimetres in all directions, a big find.

"Found something?" It was Moira. She was standing at the edge of the trench.

"Looks like a large piece of pot," David answered.

"Great!"

"With any luck I should have it clear this afternoon."

Moira nodded, looking down on him. They had known each other for years, respected each other's work, a comfortable relationship.

"Who's the new recruit?"

"Woman called Ruth. Doing archaeology as one of her Open University modules."

"Right." The name, Ruth, brought back memories. David bent over and continued the delicate probing and sweeping. Ruth, my word, yes, he thought. Was it really twenty-five years ago? In his mind's eye he saw the delicious curve of her naked hip as she lay on the bed, her back towards him, asleep on that warm afternoon in the villa. She had a delicious back, shapely, the skin smooth and fine...

Mildly taken aback by his own thoughts, David frowned and concentrated on the work. The pottery jug, for that is what he thought it probably was, was so far still intact and the area now exposed led in a curve like that now in his mind down towards the jug's shoulder. Through the dirt there were traces of colour, patterned slip. Marvelous to find so much of the vessel intact.

"Damn!" Another problem of getting older was that it was hard to remain in the same position for long; he had cramp in one leg. He hauled himself out of the trench and for a few moments danced about in pain. He smiled ruefully at the laughing faces of the three students before limping off to the Landrover, and pouring a cup of tea from the flask. Then he made his way to Moira's trench.

"You've not cleared that pot already?" she asked when she saw him.

"No, had to stop. Cramp."

"Oh." She smiled and waved a hand towards the new student, "This is Ruth Mandrill," she said, "Ruth, this is Dr Proctor, David."

Ruth turned as though startled. "Proctor?" she repeated. "David? It's not you, is it?"

They stared at one another, dumbstruck, for a few long seconds.

"Good God!" he said.

Intrigued, Moira was sitting as at a stage show, waiting for the next part of the dialogue.

"Ruth Cannings," he said.

"Mandrill," she corrected him automatically.

"It must be twenty-five years," said David.

To his surprise and her obvious confusion, Ruth blushed furiously, the colour flooding up from neck to hairline. She stood to get away from the other three occupants of the trench and climbed out, turning her face away.

"Come and have a cup of tea," said David. "It's in the Landrover."

Silently, looking at the ground, Ruth fell in beside him.

"I'm sorry if I embarrassed you," he said.

She shook her head. "Ridiculous," she said. "I don't know why I reacted as I did." But she knew. The sight of him, his name, his physical presence, towering over her in the muddy trench had recalled, unbidden, those few weeks so long ago. She had not thought of him in years. The memory she thought was dead had come to life with extraordinary vividness. It worried her, for she did not understand it, this sudden stirring of the heart, this jolt which had momentarily overwhelmed her. For a few seconds she had not been in control, had no idea what she was going to do. It was very uncomfortable.

"Of course," David said, "You're married."

"Divorced," she said. "You?"

"No, neither."

"Oh!"

"Any children?"

"Three, all grown up."

"Extraordinary what can happen in twenty-five years, I suppose."

"I married that winter," Ruth said, "Six months after you went off to Turkey."

"It was a rotten year," he said.

"Not the summer," she said, remembering.

"No, not the summer."

They reached the Landrover and drank tea, both thinking of the few months in France, when time was forgotten until David was faced with the choice of the expedition in Turkey or giving up a career he already loved. They looked at one another with a kind of wonder, looking for traces of the youth and vigour that had drawn them together in the past.

"Can we talk?" David asked. "I'll take you to dinner. What do you say?"

Ruth hesitated. "All right," she agreed.

They returned to their work, but the weather was breaking, and rain was imminent. If the work in the two trenches was not to be ruined, they would have to erect tents over them. It took the rest of the afternoon. David's jug remained two thirds buried in the soil.

"This seems unreal, doesn't it?" David said as they sat in the small restaurant that evening.

"Unreal? No, unexpected. Strange."

He nodded. Looking at her in the candle light he was finding reminders of the face he had known. The eyes still shone with amusement and kindness, the smile was the same, but there were differences, changes. There was a trace of sadness round the mouth, a slight slackness in the muscles to indicate time past, sorrows experienced. Her posture was still upright, proud, but she had put on a little weight, enough to show life had taken its toll. The curves were still there, but more ample, less vital, more relaxed. The eyes showed traces of weariness.

"You know I really loved you," he stated.

She stared back at him. "I think it was pretty obvious," she said. "It was an intense affair."

"Glorious."

"It took some time to get over it," she said.

"But you married!"

"Yes. I loved Alex," she said. "It wasn't the same. Not quite so – passionate, I suppose, slower, more satisfying in its way."

"But it didn't last."

"It lasted eighteen years. That's not bad."

"Not bad at all," he admitted.

They finished the meal like old friends. They were at ease. There was no passion, no sexual attraction now. This was not the Ruth he remembered: this was a pleasant, good-looking dinner companion. He took her home and said goodnight with a friendly kiss.

The rain eased the next day. David worked with his customary care to excavate the jug, slowly removing the rest of the soil until he reached the very bottom of the pot. The three students watched as he placed a small plastic box near the exposed find and gently began to pick away the soil, undermining it. At last he judged it would be free and with the utmost care he took the jug in two hands and millimetre by millimetre lifted it like the most fragile egg to place it on the plastic. He held his breath as he moved it. The colours were remarkable. There was silence as he placed the pot in the box and removed his hands.

There was a gasp from the watching helpers as a shard separated at the rim of the jug and dropped away from the mud inside. A second piece broke away, and a third until the entire pot was fractured by a network of cracks.

"We have good photographs," Moira said, consoling. "We can piece it all back together."

It will never be the same, thought David, remembering the few seconds when he held the jug, still whole, in his two hands. We cannot ever put it back together, not really. Picking up his trowel, he turned back to the trench.

Buster

"What have you been up to now, Ernie?" Violet, standing in the farm doorway, was looking at her husband with narrowed eyes.

"Up to? What do you mean?" he replied, assuming a look of child-like innocence.

"Don't give me that, Ernie Bloodstock. We've been married for the past fifteen years and I can tell when you've been up to something."

"Well, I ain't," he said. "And I 'aven't got time to waste dealing with your suspicious mind, Violet. It's time I was getting the cows in."

With that he turned his back and strode purposefully towards the gate of the yard. Violet watched him with a mixture of affection and amusement. He was up to something, that much was obvious, and in due course she would find out what. One of the things you learned about men when you married them was that they never really grew up. They not only expected you to mother them for the rest of their lives, but they kept the attitudes and interests they had when they were mere boys. Ernie had this childish habit of playing silly tricks and planning things in secret. She could always tell.

She turned back to her kitchen as she heard the 'phone ring. It was Betty

"Vi, are you coming to the meeting tonight?"

"The WI? Yes, I expect so."

"Oh, right, see you there, then."

"You sound fed up. You all right?"

"Yes, I'm OK. It's just that it's the Show tomorrow."

"Ah!" There was a wealth of understanding in that "Ah!" Betty's husband, Will, was a postman but he had a hobby which was close to an obsession: he kept chickens. He had always kept chickens, ever since he was a boy. It was another example of the boy who never grew up, Violet said to herself. At this time of the year, just before the Show, Will was completely unsociable and his anxiety was so clearly visible that Betty needed to keep out of his way.

Betty's house backed onto the farm and the two women were close friends. Both enjoyed being at home to look after their men and their children. None of that feminist nonsense for them. Women didn't need to prove themselves superior: after all, every day they managed the household and ran the family with far more efficiency than any man could. Unfortunately, neither of them knew how to overcome the most irritating feature in their lives: their husbands were implacable enemies. Early on, when the matter had been raised by their respective husbands, the two women had instinctively taken the same stance.

"Just because you and Ernie Bloodstock can't get on," Betty told Will, "Don't you go imagining that means I shan't stay friends with Vi. We've been good friends ever since we was at school together."

"Do as you like," he told her, "Just don't bring her here, that's all I say, not while I'm in the house, anyway."

"I wouldn't inflict you on her, Will, even with your kind permission. I think you and Ernie are stupid and obstinate. What was it made you two such enemies in the first place?"

But he never told her. Violet had similar conversations with an equally reticent Ernie. The women might never have discovered the truth were it not for the bingo.

It was Betty's idea. She suggested to Violet they might have a night out in the town, try out the bingo club. Neither had been before so it was a little adventure for them. It was pure chance that they sat next to a woman of about their own age who was good company, although the two friends found her a bit common. They talked of this and that and their new acquaintance let out a little shriek when they told her where they lived and their husbands' names.

"Ernie? Ernie Bloodstock? And Betty, you're never married to Will Mount, are you?"

"Do you know them?" Violet was amazed. This woman seemed such an unlikely person for Ernie to know.

"I knew them both. We was at school together. Tell them you met Irene Maine. Haven't clapped eyes on them for, oh, must be sixteen years or more." Feeling suddenly and uncharacteristically catty, Violet said to herself it had to be over twenty years.

"Inseparable they were, Will and Ernie, good looking in those days, too," Irene said with a dreamy look in her eyes which had Betty and Violet exchanging concerned glances. "They did everything together. Ernie's dad let him drive an old car around the farm, bought it for him. He was only about thirteen then. Oh yes, they was always tinkering about with engines. They were good mechanics, so everyone said. Ernie's dad bought him a motor bike when he was sixteen and they both passed their test. I believe Ernie lent Will his bike to take his test on

"It was about that time that I met them," Irene said, taking another sip of her rum and coke. "They both took a bit of a shine to me. You know what boys are like."

The two friends exchanged another glance, a little grim.

"What they didn't tell me was that they had a bet. They arranged a race. One of the boys from school was timekeeper. Another one waited in the square in town just over there," she pointed across the little square to the telephone box. "His job was to phone the village when the rider had got to the square. They had someone that end at that phone box. They reckoned it would take about ten minutes here and back. It's about six miles each way. Ernie had first go but no one phoned the village. They waited two or three minutes. They were wondering if he'd crashed or something, when the phone rang. It was the boy in the square here asking where Ernie had got to.

"Well, they was beginning to get worried by then, I can tell you. Some of them got on their push bikes and headed for town. There was no sign of Ernie when they got here. They rode back and looked harder in case they had missed the accident. No sign of him. One of them phoned the local hospital. There was no report of a road accident victim. We didn't know what to do but we just went home in the end. It was well after dark."

"We?" Violet asked. "Where were you, then?"

"I was in the village with the others. I told you, it was a bet. Will told me in the end."

"What sort of bet?" asked Betty.

"I was the prize. That's what they agreed between them."

"You were the prize?" Violet was shaken.

"I told you they fancied me. I thought it was all a bit daft, really."

But the two friends knew Irene was lying. Even now, twenty years later, there was a kind of smugness about her as she remembered two sixteen-year olds doing battle for her favours.

"The first Will knew was the next morning," Irene went on. "Ernie's father went to see the Mounts. He was pretty mad, so they said. He asked Will what he knew about the race. Will pretended not to know what he was talking about, then Mr Bloodstock let drop that the police had stopped Ernie on his way to town doing ninety miles an hour. Will's dad didn't believe it. But Will was so scared of his father that he went on pretending he didn't know anything about it all.

"Old Mr Bloodstock was hopping mad. Can't blame him, can you? After all he'd done for Ernie, buying the bike for him, trusting him on it, that sort of thing. It was months before Ernie talked his dad round again."

"Why did the two of them become enemies, then?" asked Violet. She wasn't sure she wanted to know the answer, especially from this stranger who knew things about both of their husbands they'd never known themselves.

"Well, as I understand it," Irene explained, her eyes alight with a kind of malicious pleasure at the memory, "Will never admitted he had anything to do with all of this, even when the police asked him. Ernie had to pay a big fine."

There was a pause before Violet asked the question they needed an answer to,,but feared. "Where did you fit in after the race, then?"

"Oh, I wasn't going to get mixed up with the law, was I? Poor old Ernie, he lost me as well as his friend. The boys I spoke to afterwards said he'd never forgive Will for dropping him in it."

"Dropping him in it!" Betty repeated, indignant.

"Well, if he'd admitted to the police they were racing for me, they might have been a bit more lenient."

The bingo finished. None of the three won anything. Violet and Betty walked out and caught the bus home, deep in a conspiratorial and angry conversation all the way to the village.

At the Village Hall Violet said hello to the other women as they filed in and placed their competition entries on the table. There was no sign of Betty, but she arrived just as the President was calling the meeting to order. Betty came and took her place by Violet. She looked flustered. It wasn't until the end of the evening, when the visiting speaker had judged the competition (the wittiest remarks on a postcard), that the two women could exchange a word.

'It's Will,' Betty said. 'Or rather, it's Buster.'

'Buster?'

'Buster, the cock; Will's entry for tomorrow.'

'Oh. What's the matter with him, fowl pest or something?' It was meant as a joke, but Violet was surprised at Betty's reaction.

'He escaped.'

'Escaped?' The very idea was a nonsense. If Buster got out of the fenced area which he shared with Will's pampered hens, he would not want to stay away for long. He knew on which side his corn was scattered.

'I think your Ernie cut the wire deliberately.'

Violet frowned. 'What for?'

'Didn't you know Ernie has put his own birds on the other side of the fence?'

'To tell you the truth, I don't go down there very often. It's got a bit muddy lately and Ernie seems happy enough to look after the hens.'

'Now you know why.'

'There's no harm done, is there?'

'Will's suicidal.'

'Why, because the bird's missing?'

'No, he came back all right, it's just that he had got through into your pen and had himself a party with your fowls.'

'So?'

'Ernie was none too particular about the state of that pen: it's ankle deep in mud. What's more you have a rooster of your own in there.'

'So we have.'

'There was a bit of a fight, not between Ernie and Will, but between the two cocks. Buster's comb is torn and his feathers are bedraggled and he has lost some; he only has half his tail feathers. There's no way Will could show him.'

'Oh dear!'

There was little sleep to be had that night in either household. Betty showed great concern and understanding for Will, who lapped up the attention, and then left for his early morning postal round at 5 am. Next door Ernie, whose glee had been dampened down like a fire by the cold-water sousing of Violet's critical words, had craved for sleep as they prepared for bed at about 10 o'clock, but been denied it as his wife had scolded and upbraided him for his callous, unfunny, childish, cruel practical joke. He was very glad to leave the house in the morning at 5.30 am for the early milking.

The two women conferred: Violet asked Betty over for coffee that morning and for once Ernie did not dare say a word, poking his head in at the kitchen door, he withdrew smartly without his morning break.

At lunchtime he was given an ultimatum: he must make it up with his former school friend or lose his conjugal rights for ever. He paled at the thought. It was not so much that he would miss his rights, more the thought of a relationship with Violet which would from now on be as implacably cold as had been his regard for Will. But he was reduced to impotence and could only surrender. His wife, pushing him to the limit, added two further clauses to the would-be contract: not only must he agree to speak to Will, but he must agree to Violet's inviting Will and Betty to a meal at the farm.

At heart Ernie was kind, a fact Violet knew very well and was counting on. For two days he held out, then he capitulated. That weekend Betty, who had called secretly the previous evening, arrived at midday at the farm with a reluctant and grim-faced Will in tow. The two men glared at one another.

'Say it, Ernie,' Violet insisted.

Ernie looked uneasily at the carpet and shifted from foot to foot.

'Well?' she prompted.

'Sorry I let your rooster out', the farmer muttered.

'What have you got to say, Will?' Betty said.

'Apology accepted,' said Will, with equal truculence.

'Will,' Violet said, 'We all know how important the County Show is to you. Betty told me that Buster's scars would mean he could never win his class again.'

'No.' The word came out as a grunt.

'Well,' said Violet, 'We thought it would be only fair if we did something about that.

'What *can* you do?'

Violet led the party outside to the barn. Inside there was a large, brand new hen coop on the floor. In the coop a bantam cock, splendid in his finery, all reds and greens, eyes glittering, stood and looked back arrogantly.

'We bought him from a breeder who specialises in showing bantams in Norfolk,' said Ernie, interested in livestock in spite of the circumstances. 'Cost us a pretty penny, I can tell you.'

Will looked at the bird with a mixture of admiration, longing and despair.

'He's yours,' said Violet.

They trooped back into the farmhouse and sat down at the table. The wine flowed, and, after a halting start, the conversation in which the men addressed mainly the women changed in tone as they began to speak to each other after twenty years' silence. They still had much in common.

As Will walked back with Betty, still warmed by the wine, he said, 'She's a good cook, isn't she?'

"Vi? Yes, she is. You enjoyed the chicken, then?'

'Yes.'

'Good. You should have. We supplied it.'

He looked at her with shock in his eyes, not daring to voice the question. She nodded. 'Well, you both had to sacrifice something to make this work,' she said. 'And don't you dare object. There wouldn't have been room for a bantam cock and Buster in the same run, now, would there?'

The Census

It's bad enough trying to run a business at the best of times, but when your country's been occupied, it gets a whole lot harder, I can tell you. You had to watch your step every moment of the day or the soldiers would just arrest you and before you knew it you'd be shut up in their blasted barracks, worrying about what was happening to your wife and your business. It's best to say nothing at all about anything, stay non-committal.

I'll say one thing for them, though, they're a thorough lot: no scruples, but then, I suppose you can even admire that in an occupying force. Any sign of rebellion and they'd come down like a ton of bricks. Crafty, too: they decided they weren't getting enough money out of us, so they decided the best thing would be to take a census: there was no avoiding it: the penalty for not registering would be death, no excuses. Not that I was complaining: it was all good business for me because everyone had to walk in from their villages to the towns and that meant they were all going to be tired, dusty and especially thirsty. I got in double the usual quantities of drink.

Sure enough we were bursting at the seams. We did a roaring trade. No one gave a toss about the quality of the wine or beer, either, so long as it was wet and alcoholic. By sunset that evening the place was absolutely heaving. My wife, Hannah, had to have her wits about her, and I needed eyes in the back of my head to watch out for thieves and layabouts, as well as for the ones who drank more than they could handle and then made a play for Hannah. I don't encourage philanderers, though I could tell you a thing or two about the Grape Leaf Inn at the other end of the street. You need only take a quick look inside at the weekend to see plenty of scruffy looking women wanting to earn a few pence the simplest way they knew.

That particular evening we were full to the eaves. It was so noisy in here you couldn't hear yourself think. One of the serving girls came up to me and said something. I couldn't hear her.

"What did you say?" I shouted. She grabbed me by the arm and pulled me out into the street. It was a bit quieter out there, but there were still lots of people about.

There was a couple standing outside. They must have travelled in from one of the villages and they looked worn out, especially the woman. She was sitting on a donkey and she was pregnant.

"We're looking for a bed for the night," the man said.

I shook my head. "Sorry, mate," I said, "Not a chance. Not a corner left. They're going to be sleeping in the main bar tonight on the benches and tables. I wouldn't be surprised if some of them end up on the floor."

"But we're desperate," he said. "You can see: my fiancée's at the end of her tether."

"Your fiancée?" I was surprised. He looked a decent sort of bloke, not one likely to saddle himself with an easy woman who'd allowed herself to get pregnant. Respectable people – and he looked pretty respectable, even if he wasn't all well off – usually followed what the Law of the synagogue said. I'm not one to condemn anyone, God knows, but fornication is a sin. I felt a bit sorry for the fool, I suppose, allowing himself to be tricked into marriage by this woman who was obviously no better than she should be. I took it for granted the child was his, but you never know for sure, do you?

"It's not the way you think," he said, seeing the look on my face. "Look, she can't go any further. When I say we're desperate, we really are. She's started labour."

That stopped me in my tracks. I scratched my head. "She can't give birth in the inn, not with all those people trampling round, most of them half cut. And we haven't got anywhere to put her – or you, for that matter."

"Anywhere," he was pleading, just managing to keep some kind of dignity. I couldn't help liking him really. "Anywhere at all," he said. "We've just got to have some kind of shelter. It's getting cold. It might even rain."

"Look, " I said, weakening, "The only place I have is out the back. It's an old animal house. The cow's out there, and a couple of donkeys and the place is filthy. You'd have to sweep the floor to make any kind of room at all. There's some clean straw in the corner."

He was almost pathetically grateful when I pointed the way round to the back courtyard. I left them to it and went back indoors. I told Hannah, of course, but for the next few hours I forgot about them until Hannah came in as I was just about to snatch a few hours sleep.

"You ought to come and see this, she said.
"See what?"
"The baby in the stable," she said. I had clean forgotten about it.
"It's been born?"
"Yes." Hannah was standing in the corner of our bedroom watching me with a funny look on her face.
"What's up?" I asked. "It's all right, isn't it? And the mother?"
"It's all right," she said, not moving. "But I think you should come and see for yourself."
"For goodness sake, Hannah! Let's get some sleep; it's been one hell of a day. Seen one baby, you've seen them all. I thought we'd had enough of babies when our last was born."

Hannah smiled at the memory: she had that curiously feminine, maternal look about her. She held out her hand. I sighed with weariness and followed her downstairs, picking the way through sleeping bodies on the floor, snoring, many of them the worse for drink. The place smelt of stale beer, wine and vomit.

Outside it was as bright as day. There was a moon and the stars shone in a clear sky – no rain after all. Overhead in the blackness of the star-pricked sky there was a strange, glowing thing, a comet, I suppose it was. It trailed a long tail from the west. It's what you might call an omen, if you believe in such things.

We headed into the stable. The woman was sleeping, the newborn baby on one arm. The man stood nearby, protective. On his face there was a curious expression that was like a kind of awe. It seems funny to describe it like that, but that's what it was like, awe. I remembered the birth of our own first child and the feelings I had experienced at the time, but even that had not produced this reaction. I looked at mother and child again.

"Boy or girl?" I asked.

"Boy," he said, as though he had known all along.

Mother and child looked surprisingly comfortable and clean. Any mess had been cleaned away. I suspected the man had been very busy, converting this outhouse into a clean, tidy, habitable place for the birth of his son. I began to feel strange, too. I don't know exactly what it was, but it was almost as if they radiated a kind of light, a sort of power. It was very still and silent. At the other side of the wooden partition of the stall, the animals were standing silently except for their quiet breathing which smelled sweet. Their hooves shuffled on the straw.

Outside in the yard came the sound of yet more arrivals. I turned to drive them away, but they had already reached the door of the shed. There were three of them, and they looked like shepherds, judging by their sheepskin cloaks and the crooks they all carried as walking sticks. The ignored me and Hannah and to my astonishment they knelt on the floor in front of the mother and child and stared. The woman woke and her movement woke her son. As he opened his eyes I felt this mysterious power hit me. I can't explain it or describe it. It just…happened. The shepherds were telling some odd story about being compelled by an irresistible force to leave the hillside and walk as though an unseen hand guided them to this stable. It was all quite bizarre and must sound like a load of nonsense, but, if you'd been there, well…

We provided them with a few extra blankets and then went to bed. The next day was busier than ever and I didn't have time to think about the couple in the stable or their curious infant son. Later that evening some of the visitors had registered for the census and had left. The inn was still full but not so overcrowded. At about six in the evening we were visited by a small cortege, almost a caravan: there were three rich looking men who'd apparently been travelling for weeks, at least according to their servants. They came from the Spice Road and, so we were told, they had known in advance about the couple in the stable. How could they, I asked. After all, they had only turned up on spec the night before. Ah, the servant said, they had followed the comet this way. It sounded more and more weird. I had no idea what they were about, but they made quite a fuss of the child, made a point of leaving him presents, and then they left.

When they'd gone, I asked the father who he was.

"Joseph," he said, "I'm a carpenter. This is Mary."

That was about all. They must have left the following day. Within a week we were back to normal. We'd done pretty well out of the census, so we weren't too bothered when things went slack for a while. We were glad of the chance of a rest, to tell you the truth.

That was the year that Herod, the Governor, decreed that all first born sons should be killed. Herod wasn't even a Roman. It was a terrible decree and the rest of the year was dreadful, everyone depressed, grieving. Some parents tried to hide their children, but the soldiers sought them out. So much for making a lot of money, I thought. It didn't make life any more agreeable in a country under military rule.

I have often wondered what happened to that strange child. I doubt if he even made it back to his village. I felt sorry for him and his parents. The odd thing is that ever since that census, I've been sort of haunted by the sense of awe and power I felt in that old shed and I've felt somehow discontented, as though I had glimpsed something truly important without knowing exactly what. Hannah and I share a glance from time to time in which I know she knows how I feel. There's something missing, and, although we comfort each other as best we can, without saying anything specific, we have this curious sense of loss…

In Sickness and In Health

The wedding photograph in its silver frame showed a handsome couple. The bride, Tanya, was dark-haired and slim. She smiled confidently at the camera, almost as if she was offering a challenge, as she clung with both arms to her husband. Jack, the groom, was also smiling, a broad, confident smile, the smile of a man who had confidence in himself and his ability to take care of the future for both of them.

Frowning, Grace Painter laid the photograph back on the sideboard and turned away. It was at times like this that being a policewoman brought a private pain which she found hard to conceal. It was silly, she knew, to allow herself to be reminded of her own disappointments and sorrows; it only distracted her from the job and flew in the face of all recommended professional behaviour. Objectivity, that was the aim. Still, it was not entirely her fault if an unexpected pebble was thrown into the placid pool of her memory and produced, unbidden, unwanted ripples of emotion. The sight of the happy newly-weds brought back the images of her own wedding day and the high hopes and the same confidence for the future as shown by Jack Cooper's expression. It was not nostalgia which filled her, however, but sadness that life could be so treacherous and confidence so misplaced: her own divorce had shattered that total belief in her future and her hopes. Why did hormones have to mislead people? Why, when intelligent thinking was clearly more realiable than impulse, did emotion seem so much more enjoyable lead you into making utterly stupid errors of judgement?

She turned from the sideboard as she glimpsed her boss, Superintendant Bloomer, in the mirror. He was coming her way.

"There's more to this than meets the eye," he said. "I'm going to spend an hour or two on all the physical evidence. I'm sure we know the how and the where. What I want to know is the why. That's your domain."

"What do you want me to do, Sir?"

"I want you to start the interview with Jack Cooper."

"Me? Are you sure you wouldn't rather wait and do it yourself, Sir? I thought he was the prime suspect."

"He is. It seems pretty clear he did it and I see no reason to change that view. What I don't understand is why. With your training in psychology and, if you'll forgive what sounds like a sexist remark, your feminine touch, I think you'll get a better idea of why he did it than I ever could."

"Right."

She liked Ralph Bloomer as much as she liked anyone these days. She was, she supposed, cynical; it was not only the police training and experience which made her so, but her personal experience and need to defend herself for ever more against the chance of further hurt. To be given the first shot at the suspect was a professional privilege and indicated Bloomer's respect for her intelligence. She left him at the scene of the crime and drove back to the station.

Before she went into the interview room, she went to her locker and found a clean blouse, washed , changed, touched up her make-up. She knew why she did this, to give herself a small breathing-space and take possession of herself once more after the disturbing sight of the murdered woman had, in spite of her attempt at dispassionate observation, left her unsettled.

Cooper was at the opposite side of the table in his wheelchair. He looked up as she came in, but his eyes lacked any feeling. The constable who had been standing just inside the door took up a new position behind the wheelchair, and sat on a chair, remaining as unobtrusive as he could. Grace opened a sealed pack of two audio tapes, taking care that Cooper could see them as she did so, and explained that the interview would be recorded. Every time she did this she was reminded of professional gamblers, opening new packs of cards before dealing the hand on which, maybe, someone's financial future depended: only in this case it was not Jack Cooper's financial future at stake, but his liberty.

She stated her name and rank, and the name of the constable, and asked Cooper to confirm his name and address. He did.

"Mr Cooper," she began, after cautioning him formally, " We are here to investigate the death of your wife, Tanya. Can you tell me what happened this morning?"

"I killed her," he said.

"Would you please tell me exactly what you did this morning, beginning at the time you woke up?"

"I woke up at about 3 o'clock."

"Is that normal?"

"Yes. I don't sleep very well."

"How long have you suffered from insomnia?"

Cooper looked at her then, mildly interested in the question. "Years," he said. "Ever since I've been disabled, I've had trouble sleeping. It's a matter of exercise, I suppose."

"You don't get enough exercise?"

"No."

"Could you not exercise the upper half of the body at least?"

"I could."

"But you choose not to."

"There is no law which says I must."

"No. So you woke at 3 o'clock. What then?"

"What do you mean?"

"Did you get up? Did you wake your wife?"

"No."

"No what, Mr Cooper? You didn't get up or you didn't wake your wife?"

"Neither."

"So did you lie there awake or did you fall asleep again?"

"I lay awake as I always did."

"Until when?"

"Until about 7 o'clock."

"What did you do all that time?"

"What do you think I did?"

"Well. did you read or listen to the radio, perhaps?"

"I just way awake, listened to Tanya breathing on the other side of the bed, and thought."

"And this was normal?"

"Yes."

Grace looked at the man opposite. The happy, smiling face in the photograph had fattened and coarsened. The eyes, not quite so dead now, were lined and tortured, and the flabby cheeks and the slight double chin sagged into a weary despair. Only the voice was alive, but it was a defensive tone he had adopted.

"So tell me what happened from the time your wife woke this morning."

Cooper looked at her without answering for a while. Then he asked, "Do you want all the details?"

"Yes, it would be best if you were as accurate as you can be."

"Tanya woke up at about seven o'clock - at exactly four minutes past, in fact. She was smiling in her sleep. When she woke up and saw me she scowled as she usually did and got up."

"Scowled? You're saying your wife always frowned at you in the morning?"

"I said scowled, not frowned, and she always looked at me that way, not just in the morning."

"Did she dislike you so much, then?"

Cooper gave a little, bitter laugh. "No more than I 'disliked' her. We had reached the stage where we hated each other."

Grace was silent a while, taking this in.

"So what next?"

"Once Tanya had completed her own ablutions and dressed, she saw to me. She helped me out of bed, into the bathroom, helped me to the toilet, dressed me, got me to my chair."

"She did this every morning?"

"Yes."

"Go on."

"I wheeled myself to the top of the stairs, got into the Stanner lift and Tanya took the wheelchair downstairs for me. Then we went into the kitchen. Tanya put the kettle on. I wheeled myself over to the work surface near the sink, took a sharp knife from the rack, and stabbed her several times until she fell to the floor. She stopped breathing. Once I was sure she was dead I phoned the police. The rest you know."

Grace looked at him. He had told the story without emotion, a factual narrative, like describing taking the dog for a walk. He looked back at her with dull eyes.

"Mr Cooper," she said, "I understand what you say, but it doesn't make sense."

"It's what happened."

"But why? Did you quarrel?"

"No."

"Then why?"

"Do you really want to know?"

"Yes."

"It's a long story."

"I'm not in a hurry."

Cooper took a long breath. "I don't know why you need to know," he said.

"Mr Cooper, unless you change your story, I

am likely to be the officiating officer who starts the process which may end in your spending the next ten or fifteen years in jail. I think I owe it to you to find out why you did what you did, and you owe it to me to explain why I am loaded with this responsibility."

"You are one of the only people I have met in the past ten years since my accident who treats me as an intelligent person and not as an object or a nuisance."

"Why did you do it, Mr Cooper?"

"I shall have to start when we first got married. I was fit then, very fit. I lived for work and sport. I was a builder, you know, and a pretty good one, too. That keeps you fit, running up and down ladders, that sort of thing. I was one of those lucky people who were reasonably bright and good with my hands and a good sportsman. I played rugby for the county in those days. In the summer I played cricket and my idea of holiday was something energetic.

"Tanya was not in my league as far as sport goes, but she was lively and enjoyed physical activities. We had fun trying all kinds of sports together, but she was also quite happy for a while to come along to watch me play this or that game. And she was a beautiful young thing. We were very much in love soon: needless to say, it was pretty physical. We were all over one another, as they say, like jelly and blancmange."

He smiled briefly at the memory. Grace glimpsed in his face the hint of the handsome young man of many years ago.

"Well, we got married. It seemed inevitable. The sex was wonderful, and it took a long time before it began to cool off at all and I began to take stock. And the first hint of a problem was about a year after we married. Tanya made it very plain she didn't want children."

"And you did?"

"I did. That wouldn't necessarily have mattered all that much. But then the relationship began to go wrong in other ways, too."

"How?"

"Oh. little things. I began to realise that Tanya was not the devoted little angel I had taken her for. She had an eye to the main chance. She saw me as a successful man who would be able to give her a life with money. Of course I did, at least to begin with. I was doing well at the work. I was self-employed and making a go of it. We had several expensive holidays. That was where I saw a bit more clearly that Tanya was not entirely devoted to me."

"She was unfaithful?"

"Not that I could prove it. She went off me, though. She began to make excuses for not sleeping with me, the old headache routine, you know, then she was never quite well. It began to worry me after a while. I was still a very active man, you realise, and I had always been - well, tactile, I suppose you might say. It wasn't just that I was in the habit of regular sex - not at all - it's just that it always came naturally to me to express myself with my hands, and physically, you know."

"Go on." Grace had some idea of what he meant.

"We had been married about four or five years when she gave up sleeping with me altogether."

"But that must have been ten years or more ago!"

"Yes."

"Why didn't you leave her, or why didn't she leave you?"

"She wouldn't leave me: I was her meal-ticket, wasn't I? I don't know why I stayed; some mistaken sense of loyalty, perhaps. I thought she had some kind of hang-up and I was arrogant enough to think, if I stuck around, I could help her shrug it off and then I should be there ready to receive her grateful body. Stupid! It never happened, of course. I simply became unhappy and threw myself into my work all the harder.

"It was during the recession by now and I had to work much harder than before to keep the work coming in and pay the bills, more and more expensive as Tanya acquired more and more expensive tastes. By now she was becoming sour and selfish and I was learning not to depend on her for anything. But more than anything I felt resentful that she had gone cold on me. I wanted to touch her, be touched, but if I so much as put out a hand she would shrug it off crossly and tell me to cut it out. When I was in financial difficulty and needed sympathy and support, all I got was rejection. And since I had, as I said, always been - well - tactile by nature, I got steadily more depressed as the physical rejection matched the emotional coldness."

"You still didn't leave?"

"Nearly. I was on the point of giving up on the whole business. I'd have given her everything I had by now just to get rid of her. I thought, if I kept my old car and my tools, she could have the rest, mortgaged house and all, and I would start all over again. But I made the mistake of telling her."

"She was angry?"

"She was more than angry. She accused me of

all kinds of betrayal and we had an almighty row. It didn't affect my decision, though. I was going to leave that afternoon."

"Why didn't you?"

"I had to fetch some of my things from the attic. I went up there to collect them and it was when I was coming down again that the ladder gave way. I fell very awkwardly, across the bannister and down the stairwell. I came to in hospital, paralysed from the waist down."

"So you couldn't leave after that."

"I was pretty helpless. I couldn't work for a long time and, since it was an accident in the home, there was no way I could claim any kind of insurance."

"And your wife?"

"She couldn't leave, could she? It wasn't that she felt in any way obligated to me, but she had nowhere to go and no money of her own."

"I understood she did get a job later."

"Oh yes, she did; much later. At first she stayed and looked after me - more or less. Her parents would have taken a dim view if she simply walked out, but she became even more bitter. She continually asked me why I hadn't died in the accident so she could at least have had the insurance."

"Couldn't you have arranged something else? Gone back to live with your own parents, perhaps?"

"They were both dead."

"So she stayed with you after all and looked after you like a dutiful wife."

"Yes. 'like' a dutiful wife; she wasn't really."

"I don't understand," said Grace. "You insist she didn't love you, yet she stayed and looked after you for the next ten years. She had to support you after a while, I understand?"

"Yes. She got a job in a travel agents."

"She sounds like a dutiful wife to me. It can't have been easy for her, looking after a disabled husband she didn't love."

"Oh, I think she suffered quite a lot in the end. The job was not just for the money; it gave her an excuse to leave the house, get away from me but she soon found she hated that, too. All those expensive holidays she couldn't afford."

"So much bitterness! Why did you have to kill her?"

"Can't you begin to imagine what it has been like for me? I used to be physically active, enjoying sport and work. My major frustration was lying in bed feeling sexually rejected. Suddenly, here I was confined to a wheelchair and having to have my every personal need seen to by Tanya; her hands on my body, all over it, dressing and undressing me, washing me, bathing me, none too tenderly, either. Have you the least idea of the humiliation involved? For ten long years I have been physically dependent on the person I loathed . Every morning I woke at 3 am and lay beside her, hating her, unable to move."

"But what tipped the balance this morning? What drove you to kill her?"

"It was something she said last night. We had another row; she was talking about a lover she said she had, another one. I don't know what it was I said this time to provoke her but she slipped up for the first time in ten years."

"What do you mean, 'slipped up?'"

"For the first time ever she admitted what I had suspected all this time."

"You are talking in riddles, Mr Cooper."

"I'll spell it out for you then. The accident was no such thing."

"What are you saying?"

"That afternoon when I climbed into the attic, Tanya had undone the bolts securing the bottom half of the loft ladder. She meant it to give way."

"Are you sure?"

"Oh yes! She told me; she screamed it at me last night. She had wanted me to fall and break my neck. All these years she had been living with me with that on her conscience. That's too strong a word for it. She was scared all the time that the truth would come out; that's really why she stayed."

"But to kill her!"

"No one would ever believe my story and she would never admit it again, would she? And if she was punished having to look after me all those years, I hadn't been properly avenged, had I?"

Grace switched off the recorder and stood up. She looked down an the man in the wheelchair with mixed emotions. He had lived in a hell of his own for the past ten years; he would now almost certainly spend several more years in jail but his surroundings would be of no consequence to him. In effect his life had ended many years ago, or at least his happiness had.

"Are you all right?" Superintendant Bloomer asked.

"I think so."

"Well done. Sounds as though you have it all wrapped up."

"Makes me glad I'm not married any more."

"Poor sod!" he said. "He's right, of course, no one would ever have believed his wife tried to kill him. Still, his defence might make something of it."

"I'm off," said Grace. "I think I shall go home and have a bath, try to wash some of the smell away. Then I'll watch a bit of telly. I hope there's something not too serious to watch."

"Funny old life, isn't it?" said the superintendant. "I was going to paint the upstairs windows tomorrow. Now I think I'll wait till the wife's on holiday. Goodnight."

Later, lying in the bath, Grace found herself thinking about Colin, her "ex", for the first time in months. They had found their interests and enthusiasms came between them and agreed to part without regrets but, - and for this she was suddenly grateful - she could not hate him, and if their separation had brought her sadness and disillusionment, it had left them both with enough energy to want to pursue life. And, for a moment, she felt a touch of affection for him. She smiled, then stood up and reached for the towel.

The Return

Old Matthew, propping up the corner of the bar in the Lamb and Flag as he had for the past fifty years, listened with interest as the visitor spoke to John Bright, the landlord.

"I'm Sam Tregunna," said the newcomer. "You've got a room for me, I think." South African, wondered Matthew, no, probably Australian. But the name, Tregunna, that rang a bell. He looked at the newcomer more intently.

Sam Tregunna was tall, slim, bronzed and in his fifties. He had a self-confident, sombre air.

"Give me ten minutes," John said, "Then I'll take you up to your room. Would you like a drink?"

"You're not Arthur Tregunna's boy, are you?" asked Matthew, attracting the man's attention.

"Did you know him?"

"Oh yes!" Matthew said nothing more for a moment or two, then, "Didn't expect to see a Tregunna back in Bosventon. Not since your dad went off to Australia."

"New Zealand."

"Oh, yes, New Zealand. I haven't seen you since you were knee high to a grasshopper."

"You remember us?"

"I remember all of you. That's why I'm surprised you've come back."

The silence between them was thick with unspoken memories. Matthew was thinking of the bitter departure. He had shared a desk with Arthur Tregunna in the village school, before Arthur left for the war, while Matthew, needed to help run his father's farm, stayed in the village. Arthur returned to discover just how his young wife had been persecuted in his absence. Matthew had been only too ready to join the rest of the villagers in their mistrust of the German in their midst.

"How old were you when you left?" he asked. "Six?"

"Seven."

"And what brings you back, curiosity, is it?"

"No. My father's funeral."

Consternation on Matthew's face: "He's dead?" But it wasn't all that surprising after all. Arthur was almost exactly his age, seventy-five. "Where.?"

"Where did he die?" Sam completed the question. "In New Zealand," he said. "But he wanted to be buried here, in Bosventon. He wrote it in his will."

"I'm sorry, boy," said Matthew. He was confused. Why would anyone with painful memories of the place want to go to the trouble of arranging for his body to be transported halfway round the world?

"What did he tell you about us?" he asked.

"Quite a bit."

"Is your mother here?"

It seemed a casual question, but underlying it was, Matthew realised, a growing need on his part to tell Marthe he was sorry. He wanted to atone somehow for the small-minded, cruel way he and the other villagers had behaved all those years ago. In his imagination he saw her now, a pretty face, but always drawn, always lonely. She took her small son to school every day where he was taunted and bullied because his mother was German. She kept herself to herself. Even had she wanted to mix with the rest of the village, she would not have been able to, because people turned their backs when she passed, fell silent when she entered the village shop, sat separately in the little church as they prayed for victory over the Germans.

Sam was looking at him with surprise. "My mother?" he repeated, "She died a year after we got to New Zealand."

Another silence.

"Did your father remarry?"

Sam shook his head. It was his turn to remember. His father must have suffered terribly. He had returned to the village only to fight another war on Marthe's behalf. It had seemed kinder, fairer to her to leave. Their two brief years' happiness before war intervened were forgotten, but now there was a chance of starting again.

His wife contracted tuberculosis, perhaps already was infected when they arrived in their new home. Her death, when it came, devastated both father and son. Sam at least had his school to occupy him where, in contrast to the miserable bullying he had suffered in Bosventon, he was treated with kindness, made friends, began to enjoy being with other children. His father, bitter from his loss, suffered a depressive illness which lasted years.

He had never been particularly religious but now he railed against a cruel god. He felt terribly alone. His salvation lay in providing for his son as he grew up. He started a small radio and television business. It did well, but he took no pleasure in it.

Sam left school, took over the business, made it truly prosperous.

Very late in life Arthur had gone back to the church, found, finally, a degree of comfort. Even so, Sam had not known, until he read his father's will, that he had made detailed arrangements for his own funeral, arrangements which perplexed him. A year before he died Arthur had contacted the vicar of Bosventon and booked a plot in the little churchyard. He even contacted an undertaker in nearby Penzance and investigated the problems of transporting a coffin from New Zealand so that the formalities were comparatively simple to arrange. Sam had little choice but to honour his father's request.

His own memories of the village were remote and overlaid by many years of far happier experiences. Now, a stranger in a remote Cornish village which had given the entire family only pain, he wanted to get the funeral over with and get away.

"When's the funeral?" asked Matthew.

"Tomorrow at three."

"Have you brought many people with you?"

Sam looked at him sharply, suspecting this was a form of irony. "No," he said. "The rest of the family is back in New Zealand. We arranged a memorial service there. I'm not sure this is a good idea. Bosventon wasn't kind to my father."

"He was Cornish," Matthew said, as though that explained everything. "It's only right that he should come home."

The following day was overcast with a chill, autumnal wind. Sam arrived as the clock struck two and took his place in the front pew. He wanted time to think. So far, his grief had not surfaced, merely a sense of regret. He looked around him. Bosventon Church was undistinguished and gloomy. As he sat in the damp, chill air, he read the small plaques on the walls, commemorating past incumbents.

He expected the service to be difficult. The vicar, the sexton, and four bearers provided by the undertaker would be the only mourners apart from himself. There was nothing to say, just bare ritual.

Fifteen minutes before the service Sam heard footsteps. He did not look round. A little later he heard more footsteps and he turned to see three elderly people sitting near the back of the church. He was surprised. By five minutes to three, there were ten women, five men, one of them Matthew, the man he had met in the Lamb and Flag. Matthew inclined his head gravely in salutation.

At three o'clock precisely the vicar entered by the west door, leading the four bearers with the coffin. The service began with dry words to formalise the departure of Arthur Tregunna.

The vicar paused in the ceremony and announced, "Matthew Jenkins has a few words to say." Sam looked up in surprise as the old man stepped forward to the lectern. He had a sheet of paper in his hand.

"This village," he read, in a firm voice, "did Arthur Tregunna a great wrong and an even greater wrong to his wife, Marthe. We wish to make a public statement before it is too late and to offer his son, Sam, our apologies and ask his forgiveness.

"During the war we were all fighting the Nazis but we made the mistake of thinking that all Germans were tarred with the same brush. We treated Marthe Tregunna not only as a foreigner but as an enemy. We were wrong. Our behaviour made her life wretched and made young Sam's life miserable as well.

"When Arthur returned from the war, from fighting these same Nazis, we let him see only too clearly what we thought of his choice of wife. We judged Marthe unjustly, and we drove Arthur from his home and his birthright.

"This statement is a public acknowledgement of our error. We shall publish it in the local press next week with the names of the surviving villagers as signatories. A local artist is making two copper plaques, one of which will be mounted in this church, one will be given to Sam Tregunna to take back to New Zealand for the parish church where his father worshipped. The inscription on the plaque reads in Cornish and in English:

"Gaf dhyn agan camwul. Pobl Bosventon."

"Forgive us our trespasses. The villagers of Bosventon."

As he stood at the graveside, surrounded by the villagers in their funeral clothes, Sam looked down at his father's coffin and, for the first time since the death, his tears flowed as he muttered, "Rest in peace, father. You're home at last."

Visiting Father

"You'll have to go and see him," Kay said.

Mike looked at her as she gazed at him from the pillow. She was tired, unable to sleep, disturbed by his anxiety.

"It won't help," he said.

"I know you find it difficult to talk to him.."

"Difficult! It's impossible. Always has been."

"But he is your father. You have to try."

He sighed. This was familiar ground. He turned on his back and lay, wide-eyed in the near-darkness.

"Tomorrow," Kay insisted. "Try, Darling, for my sake, for your sake, for all our sakes, please!" She kissed him lightly. "Get some sleep, Mike. No sense in making us both more tired than we already are."

He turned back to her at that, took her in his arms, found comfort in her warmth.

"All right," he said, his voice muffled, his mouth close to her ear. "I'll go. Don't suppose it'll achieve anything. I'll ask him. He'll say no. I'll come home. He won't take the risk"

"Just try," she said.

As he got out of the car his father was outside the door of the little bungalow. He had seen him arrive and come out to meet him. Mike walked down the six steps that led from the footpath. They shook hands. His father turned and led the way indoors.

Nothing had changed. The living room was shabby, dominated by a table in the middle. There were the same armchairs either side of the electric fire. The television set stood on a rickety table in one corner. In the other, books filled the wall from floor to ceiling, a job lot. Some were stacked flat on top of others. They all looked dusty.

"I'll make some tea," said his father, and went into the adjoining kitchen to fill the kettle, make a pot of tea, set out some biscuits on a plate.

Mike sat down in his mother's chair. Not for the first time since she died two years ago he wondered how his father must feel, sitting alone in this room they had shared for twenty years, then shuffling into his bedroom to sleep alone. He would never know, because his father would not be able to tell him, even if he wanted to. He was not in the habit of sharing his feelings, had not done so with his wife, never with his son.

"Well, now," he said, setting the tray down. "What's the news?"

"News?"

"I don't imagine you've just driven all the way here without Kay just to say hello," said his father. "You must have something you want to tell me."

Mike felt uncomfortable at this directness. He sipped the tea. "Well, I do have some news of a kind," he admitted. "Not exactly news. It's more something I want your advice on."

"My advice!" The old man raised his eyebrows with a touch of humour at his discomfiture. "Don't expect my advice will be much use to you."

"Dad - this is difficult!"

"Difficult? What's up, Michael? You're a successful man in your own right. How on earth can you need my advice?"

Mike took a deep breath. "I've been offered a new job," he said.

"Oh?"

"I don't know whether to take it or not."

"But I don't know anything about your work!" This was not, Mike knew, quite the truth. His father had taken enormous pains to read up as much as he could about muscular distrophy, borrowed books from the library, ordered them, struggled hard to follow with carefully hidden pride the research his son was carrying out at his university department.

"It's a good job," Mike said. "It would mean leaving London, though, and working for a private company."

"That's bad, is it?"

"Not in itself, no. The research is just the same only there's more money available, better equipment, that sort of thing."

"Sounds too good to be true."

"It's overseas," Mike said, watching for his father's reaction.

"Where overseas?"

"The USA. Baltimore."

"Risky?"

"Well, no," said Mike, again uncomfortable that his father was asking all the questions but contributing little. "There's nothing wrong with it. It's a very solid company, well established and respected."

"So why are you asking me about it? I don't know anything; you know that."

"Dad, you know what I'm talking about. If I took this job, Kay and I would have to move abroad to live. The contract is for a minimum five years."

"What does Kay think?"

"She'd love it."

"So what's the snag? I can see there might be a problem later, if you wanted to come back to the UK"

"No, not at all. This would if anything be good for my career, even if I wanted to come back. There's not really a snag at all."

"You know, Michael, you have annoyed me over the years, ever since you were knee-high to a grasshopper."

"Annoyed you, Dad? How?"

"Well, everyone seems to think you're a clever sort of chap. I mean, you did well at school, didn't you? Then you went on to Cambridge, sailed through that, got a good degree. Now you seem to be making a name for yourself in your line of research. I saw that paper you wrote with Dr Chartis in the Lancet last month."

"What were you doing with the Lancet?"

"You mentioned the paper some time or other. I like to keep up," his father almost mumbled, as though ashamed at being caught out this way.

"And did you understand it?"

"Some of it. Most of it was over my head. Still, it looked important."

Mike didn't reply. This had always been the way their relationship had gone; he was never sure if his father was proud of him because he never said so.

"You said I have annoyed you over the years," Mike said. "You haven't said how."

"It's the way you start to say something but then can't spit it out. You said you came here to ask my opinion about a new job, but you've just told me there's nothing wrong with it, no snags, it's perfect. I have no idea what you want me to say."

"Oh, Dad, you know what the problem is."

"I do?"

"Yes. If Kay and I take off for five years in the States, you'd be on your own here, completely."

"I'm on my own anyway, have been ever since your mother died. I've lasted two years. I dare say I can last another ten, maybe twenty."

"No one's suggesting you can't cope, Dad. It's just that...' He hesitated, knowing what he had to ask would be pointless. 'Look, how would you feel about coming with us?"

The old man looked him straight in the eye, frowning, as though trying to assess the sincerity of the invitation. Then he shook his head.

"It wouldn't work," he said.

"Why not? I'll earn a lot more in Baltimore. We could afford to buy a place with proper accommodation for you. Kay would love you to be with us. You know that."

"She's a fine lass," his father acknowledged. " She's the best thing that ever happened to you, lad. You don't deserve her."

Mike was nonplussed to be called "lad". It was like a gruff attempt, the merest hint of affection. It has slipped out unconsciously.

"So why don't you come with us?" he asked, but he knew the answer. It would be taking a chance. The one thing the old man had never been able to do. Always conscious of the risks that surrounded him, he hedged himself in with every precaution, from insurance to burglar alarms.

"All kinds of reasons."

"What are they?"

"For a start I'd have to leave this place."

Mike looked round at the scruffy little room, its worn-out furniture, its pathetic collection of books, cheap ornaments and bric-a-brac.

"You could bring anything you wanted to your new home," he said.

"Mike, let's be honest with each other. It wouldn't work."

"Why not? We don't spend all our time in arguments or anything."

"I'm an old man, living with my memories."

"Young enough to make a new start. You're only sixty-five."

"Yes, but you aren't."

"I don't follow you."

"You and Kay are starting out on life," his father said. "I'm setting out on the last part of mine. I don't any longer want the burden of the future."

"Burden of the future? What on earth do you mean?"

"You need energy to cope with the future, to see it as a challenge to be looked forward to. Every day at your age you wake up and forget yesterday, look forward to solving today's problems. Not me. I wake up and look back. Most of the time with gratitude, sometimes with regret. I need the comfort of familiar things, of familiar places, of familiar faces, and I need to be close to my memories."

"Dad," Mike said, moved in spite of himself, "Mum has been dead for two years now. You can't bring her back."

"Don't you think I know that?" His father spoke sharply, putting him in his place as though he were still a child. "I don't sit here and wallow in nostalgia, Michael, I'm not that stupid. The fact is that I am plain tired. I can't be doing with too much novelty, too much challenge. But worse than that, I don't think I want to spend my life constantly fitting into your family, with you, with Kay and later on with your children. I want to be independent."

"You'd have your independence."

"I'd be tied to you."

Mike got up from the chair and turned to the window. Outside the sun had gone, replaced by grey skies. The garden was rather overgrown, he said to himself.

"I'm not sure I want to go and leave you behind," he said.

"You see," his father said, "It's not really much fun for you being tied to me, either, is it? You go, Michael, you and Kay. I can always come to visit you."

"I know you," his son said with a mixture of resignation and bitterness. "You won't get on a plane."

"You might be surprised." His father surprised him with a smile. "I could always take out travel insurance."

Mike laughed out loud.

"I know how I must seem," his father went on. "You think I'm a pathetic old man who won't take risks."

Mike did not reply. He couldn't believe what he was hearing.

"In a sense," the old man went on," You are right. Life has not always been easy, you know. I have always felt it was more responsibility than pleasure, I suppose. And being cautious becomes a habit." He picked up the photograph of him and his wife, the two of them arm in arm, in their best clothes, in the garden before the children had been born. They looked steadfast, serious, even then. "I only see the possible problems in the future. I can't help it."

"There will always be problems," said Mike gently.

"I know." He put down the photograph and was silent for a while. "All the same," he said, "moving to another country at my age would be courting disaster. I wouldn't be happy. You know it really."

"We can't leave you here alone."

"Nonsense! I'm a grown-up, Michael, not a child, just as you are. For you this is a decision you can't not make. I don't even come into the equation. And I mean it when I say I can always come and visit. I think I'd like that."

They walked into town together as far as the Golden Lion. Mike bought lunch and they talked of uncontroversial things, of the local football team, of the new building in town, of people they both knew. They avoided further talk of the family.

Mike left at about four o'clock.

"Bring Kay with you next time," his father said.

"I will."

"Michael, before you go.."

Mike looked at him, puzzled. His father was struggling to express something.

"I've never said this to you before," He looked distressed, embarrassed, as though he were about to betray some well-kept, dark secret from decades ago. Then he put a hand on the car door, while Mike looked up at him anxiously. "Michael, I want you to know I'm proud of you, proud of what you have achieved. I don't find it easy to say these things. I think you know that. People of my generation, well, we just never talked about feelings. But that doesn't mean - well, you know what I'm trying to say."

"Dad, thank you. I don't know if I've ever said as much to you, either, but I have always been proud of you, too."

They looked at one another for several seconds, then, clearing his throat, Mike turned on the engine and let in the clutch. Behind him his father half raised a hand in salute until the car disappeared round the corner, then, shoulders drooping, he turned back to the house where he began to clear away the cups and saucers.

Kay looked at him as he came in. She did not recognise the look on his face. "Well?" she asked.

"He told me we should go. I asked him to come with us. He said no."

"What you expected, then."

"No, not exactly. We...he...we actually *talked* to each other." His face was such a confusion of emotions that Kay simply took him in her arms like a baby.

"I never realised," he admitted later, "how painful talking can be. For Dad, it must have been even harder. He said he had become cautious by nature and only saw problems. To admit your feelings like that is to take a huge risk of being hurt. He thinks the world of you, you know."

"He does?"

"He said as much."

"My goodness!" Kay had an image in her mind of a careworn old man, reserved, who had looked embarrassed when he had kissed his son's bride. "You must have had a real heart to heart."

"We did." The look of wonder remained on Mike's face. "You know, he even said he would fly out to Baltimore to see us."

"So we're definitely going?"

"We're going."

And in his eyes Kay saw a new kind of peace, the kind which only comes when anxieties, long felt, begin to melt away like snow in the spring.

The Lantern Room

It was some two months after his mother's death that Jason received details of the lighthouse. It was a comparatively small property, built on the end of a promontory and now disused. It had only four stories with one room on each floor. The ground floor was a storage room and scullery with a bathroom. On the floor above there was a kitchen-diner, well appointed. The third storey, once the lantern room, was entirely glass and was used as a sitting room with the most extraordinary views all round. The bedroom was a slightly smaller room above that. The middle two floors were obviously where one was expected to live.

Jason had himself driven out to inspect it. He insisted on seeing it without the agent, telling him he would phone him with his decision. The seclusion was not total, since the promontory was a wild but public space with a footpath which led some two miles from the nearest village and looped round the cliff-edge before leading off again in the other direction, but the path itself was yards away and walkers would, Jason presumed, be more interested in scanning the sea and the horizon as they circled his lighthouse, than in looking at the building itself. He was more concerned at the time with the outlook for himself, than the threat of visitors.

On his return that afternoon he rang the agents. "I'll take it," he said. He could only bear to talk to people on the phone if it was strictly essential.

He moved in towards the end of summer.

He busied himself with all the necessities of living. He would need no one to look after him here and proposed to do his own housekeeping. He had a telephone installed so that he could order supplies rather than having to visit the town. He selected sufficient furniture to meet his needs and had it delivered while he stayed away, getting the estate agent, rather to his surprise, to supervise its installation for a substantial extra fee. He explained clearly where the heaviest items were to be set up; smaller pieces he could arrange for himself.

"You do realise," said the agent, "that there is not even a television aerial?"

"Fine," said Jason, "I don't want one."

He did not have a radio, either.

It was a wet summer and the day he left his mother's house it was raining hard. Jason took a taxi to his new property. He had told the taxi firm the destination and the time and found no need to speak to the driver who tried to make conversation as he opened the car door. Instead Jason climbed into the back seat and sat silently. He did not so much as look round as the car hesitated at the end of the drive and pulled away for the last time. He found the necessity of driving through traffic, sharing the road with other people, irksome. Arriving at the lighthouse he did not look at the driver when he unloaded the two suitcases from the boot. He simply handed him two ten-pound notes and, when the man said, "Sorry, Guv, but I haven't got change for this; the fare was agreed: £14 for the trip," he did not meet his eye, but waved dismissively and the man, grateful for the unexpected tip and glad to get away from his strange fare, hastily drove off.

Jason, relieved to be on his own again, let himself into the lighthouse and carried his cases up three flights of stone steps to the bedroom. He took a brief look at the kitchen, noting the general disarray. His first task would be to sort it out. He paused very briefly in the lantern room. He felt uneasy and exposed. The room was not exactly circular, for the walls of glass were actually flat,and there were 32 of them, plain, thick windows, giving the illusion of a round room. The sitting room furniture was dumped here, chairs, settees, one or two small tables, bookcases. In the very centre of the room there was an open hearth. There were no curtains. It would have been a huge task to curtain the entire room and pointless to curtain only a part of it. Four of the glass walls were in fact sliding doors which allowed egress onto the balcony that ran the entire circuit. Among other advantages, it meant that cleaning all the glass was made easier.

But Jason was not keen to stop here, and he carried his suitcases up one more flight of steps to the bedroom and unpacked. Here there were four windows, but they were all curtained and there was more wall area than glass. He felt safer.

Once he had unpacked and made up the bed, Jason made his way back downstairs to the kitchen, not pausing in the lantern room. When he had first seen the building, he had realised this was a room he would not use very much or at all. It was too much like living in the open, although it was set eighteen feet above the surrounding grass. He had no great wish to stare out, since it meant any passer-by could just as easily see him. He intended to use the kitchen as a living area and foresaw the lantern room would be merely a space through which he would pass on the way to and from the bedroom. It was also a convenient room in which to store some of his belongings.

He took up residence in the comfortable kitchen. He was busy at first simply sorting out his affairs. He had brought with him some of his mother's possessions, including the contents of her writing desk and half a dozen photograph albums. There were also several boxes of papers and letters which he would sort at his leisure.

The rain continued throughout his first week and he was largely unaware of it as he busied himself unpacking and putting away kitchen utensils, clothing, supplies. In the lantern room he left the books and papers in piles, the bookcases empty. They were not in his way as he made his way to and from the bedroom. He had brought the old, deal table for the kitchen and this made a good workbench on which he sorted the papers. By the kitchen stove he sat and read.

It was on the third or fourth day that he paused briefly on his way to the bedroom and looked at the windows of the lantern room for the first time. The rain was fine, more like low cloud, obscuring the view so that he could see only a few yards of grass and heather. The cliff path was not visible. Inside the house he had not turned on a light and he realised it was even darker inside than out, so that a passer-by, should there be one, would not see him through the reflected light in the windows. Inside his glass tower Jason walked round the room and peered out. He could see nothing but damp grass and heather. He felt comfortably secure. The rain appeared to be condensing on the glass rather than striking it, a mist which covered the whole surface and then began to coalesce into larger droplets which ran together and formed trickles than stopped, started, hesitated, ran down to the sill. The image of the world outside was distorted by these rivulets of rain-water. Jason sat down in an armchair, not bothering to move the dust-cover, and watched the rain on the windows with a dull fascination.

Later that same evening, on his way to bed, he paused again. It was dark inside the room and he was totally invisible to the outside world. The rain had eased and he could now just make out the cliff edge and the light grey of the sea under the darker grey of the low cloud. Nothing moved. It was as though he were in a dead, deserted world. It calmed him and almost numbed his senses. After a while he went on to bed.

Apart from necessary forays to fetch more papers or books, Jason did not spend time in the lantern room again for several days. Showers took the place of the drizzle, showers of heavier rain which lashed the lighthouse and obscured the windows, but when they stopped there were bright intervals in which a fitful sun shone. Now the horizon was where the sea met the sky and there was a pearly luminescence over the water in the morning and evening which, like a fluorescent strip lit up the interior of the lantern room as well. Jason hurried through it. On one occasion as he did so he realised the room smelled stuffy and he slid open one of the windows.

"It's no longer in use." A man's voice floated up from below the walls. Jason froze.

"It's very romantic." A woman's voice this time.

"Pretty isolated, though. Don't think I'd like it."

"Typical! Always practical. No soul, have you?" But it was said with a light laugh.

"Come on, we'll be still walking in the dark if we don't get a move on."

Jason, flat against the wall of the lantern room felt a sudden pang of anxiety seize him when he saw the brilliant yellow of two anoraks as the walkers strode off towards the cliff path. The sight of a human being, the first for some five days, was enough to make him feel threatened, even though they had their backs to the lighthouse. No one, Jason realised, would walk this path without at least a curious look in the direction of the building. He did not want to be seen.

Yet from his bedroom windows, protected by the curtains, he was able to look out and watch the sea and the birds. Sitting thus on a chair by the window, he was able to watch the top of the cliff while remaining completely out of sight of any casual passer-by. When the showers gave way to a period of sunny weather, he spent several hours each day in this position. The only problem it presented was having to pass through the sunny lantern room to get to the kitchen or bathroom. He dashed across the space as though the sun might damage his skin, and closed the door at the top of the kitchen stairs with the same kind of haste as a child runs across a pavement, avoiding the cracks between the stones. He loved watching the gulls as they soared over the cliffs, riding the updraft. They made so little effort. He admired the pure white of their plumage and the nonchalant skill with which they cried to one another and moved their heads, even scratching themselves in flight as though their outstretched wings were automatic devices. He watched them come in to land on the edge or on small ledges, timing their approach to perfection to arrive a matter of an inch or two above their perch, then spilling the air from their wings to land as delicately as thistledown.

He took to watching the sea, too, but this was less rewarding. The inanimate waves rolled in with a somehow frightening power, reminding him by their eternal yet lifeless motion of his own impermanence. All the same, on rough days his eyes were drawn to the explosions of spray as the big waves thundered against the cliff to his left. And he was able to watch small ships, coasters, making their way along the coast slowly and silently, too far off to be thought of as connected with human beings. The boats were things in their own right, struggling against the equally inanimate sea.

When it began to get dark he felt safe in the lantern room. Provided he did not put on a light or put a match to the fire, it was darker inside than out, and no one could possibly see him. On one such occasion, after a squally day, the rain ceased for a while but threatened to return. Heavy clouds rolled in from the horizon, lightning flashing in and beneath them. It was a spectacular show which came gradually closer as the darkness fell. By dusk the storm was very close and wild. The thunder was loud, shaking the windows in the bedroom, but having no effect on the thickened glass of the lantern room. Sheet lightning lit up whole ranges of clouds as though stage lighting was being used to set a spectacular scene for a Wagnerian opera. The clouds were backlit and silhouetted briefly. Forked lightning streaked down from the underside of the clouds to the sea and the thunder clap which followed was a deafening crack. The storm came closer and closer until it was above and around him. One flash of lightning was so bright that he could see nothing for a startled moment, but his own figure reflected in the glass outside; the lightning struck the conductor on the top of the lighthouse and he saw the raw power of it course down the thick copper conductor which ran down the outside of the window, crackling and burning as it went. He found it absolutely thrilling.

But it was his image, illuminated by the flash of lightning which remained in his memory afterwards. It was the image of a thin man with a beard. He stood transfixed and stared, his black eyes lit by the reflected flash. His mouth was open and white teeth gleamed in a snarl. His hair, black and long, added a further touch of wildness. And since he was standing in a comparatively empty part of the room, this image was entirely alone, imposed on a black background.

The experience of the storm led him to visit the lantern room frequently at and after dusk. It was a long time before he felt comfortable there, however. He came to realise after some weeks that the cliff path was very rarely visited even by walkers and then it was in the middle hours of the day. In fact he only saw four ramblers in the first six weeks; they were walking purposefully along the path and in every case it was after ten in the morning and before three in the afternoon. Jason took to spending more time in the lantern room then and, as the days grew shorter and colder, he lit the fire. The balcony which ran round the lighthouse at this level meant that his view of the outside world began some fifty yards from the building and by the same token, no one any closer would be able to see inside. Even so he sat well away from the glass.

One evening as he sat thus with the fire burning redly in the centre of the room he watched the sun set over the sea. It was a dark, deserted scene, hardly a bird in the sky, no ships, the sombre skies unmoving. And as he watched he realised the fire was reflecting in the glass and, as he focused his gaze, he saw his own image again, this time very dark, like an old oil painting on which the varnish had darkened and obscured the original work. He moved an arm and saw a corresponding move in the glass. Shifting his gaze to another area of the wall he was able to see a different image. It was like one of those triple mirrors you can find on dressing tables. Because the thirty-two windows were all at slightly different angles to his position, he saw as many images when he looked hard. He became intrigued and searched for the differences.

After a while this became a favourite occupation just after dark. He had begun to lose track of time. It had no significance for him. He remembered, since he had established a routine, to phone through his orders for supplies and he was always on edge every morning in case the postman called. Once a week a dustcart bumped its way down the rocky track that led to his tower and the men emptied his bin. Otherwise he saw no one; the grocer who drove to him with his van left his cardboard boxes of supplies outside the door. Jason waited until he had gone before bringing them in.

The lantern room with its images began to entrance him. To give himself more courage to risk exposure he began to take a drink before climbing the steps from the kitchen. He found the mildly numbing effect helped him face the darkness of the windows and their multiple images beyond which lay another kind of unseen reality. One drink led to another until he regularly took three or four glasses of whisky during the afternoon before he lit the fire in the lantern room fireplace.

It was some time before he began talking to the images in the glass. He found he saw each one not only as a different facet, but as a different personality after a while. To distinguish them one from another he gave them different names. There was the stern man who stared straight back at him from immediately in front of his chair. He was Genghis, short for Genghis Khan. Over to the right sat David, the quiet philosophical type, his arm movements echoing his observations. To his left was Sydney, a bit of a coward. Jason began holding conversations with his companions until one day he found they not only spoke to him, but to each other too.

"Jason," sneered Genghis, "What kind of name is that?"

"Jason was the leader of the Argonauts," replied David.

"And who were they?" Genghis pursued.

"Greek warriors - sailors."

At this Genghis began to laugh his cruel, harsh laugh. "You a warrior!" he howled at Jason.

"He's only called Jason," a pale, effeminate image, Helena, said softly. "And there are other virtues than physical courage."

"Rubbish!" shouted Genghis.

"Understanding, compassion, things you know nothing about," this from St Francis, whose dark beard contrasted with a pale, suffering face.

David cut in. "Not everyone respects bullies, Genghis."

"Bullies? Bullies? Who do you think you are talking to?"

"You are remembered with horror as a model all children should avoid copying," David said.

"Can't we all talk about something less controversial?" Sydney pleaded.

"What do you think, Jason?" David said.

"Yes," Helena added. "We all realise you have your tender side. You don't have to be macho with us."

Unable to control them, Jason became alarmed at the arguments and threats as they postured and cowered. like a pack of wolves establishing the order of supremacy. But since, even from within the veil of alcohol which protected him, he still knew they were all parts of him, he was more and more frightened. He tried to stop using the lantern room for a while, but then there was a feeling of terror every time he passed through it on his way to or from his bedroom, as though the ghostly images, unseen during daylight hours, were hiding from him and watching him spitefully, resentful that he had sent them temporarily into exile. They were, he felt, invisible but still there, and becoming more and more malevolent in their resentment.

As October passed into November, the fogs arrived. Now Jason knew for sure he was isolated. Outside the windows nothing was visible but a swirling, white screen on which the images screamed at him to be projected so that they could resume their bickering. He resisted as long as he could with the aid of more bottles of whisky, then he gave in, seeking a peace which he did not find. Instead he found the opposite, a hell of internal argument and fighting.

"You pathetic apology for a man!" snarled Genghis. "You can't even decide who you are."

"It's not his fault," Sydney said, "Leave him alone."

"You stupid wimp!"

"Ignore him, Jason," said Helena. "We all understand."

"Turn to God," said St Francis. "It's the only way you'll find peace."

"You need to find yourself," said David. "Yourself."

"How do I do that?" Jason asked, despairing.

"You can't," Genghis bared his teeth in the

glass as the fire flared behind him. "You don't have the guts to live with yourself."

"Why don't you leave me alone?" Jason cried, waving the bottle at the image.

But Genghis was threatening him with a huge club, his dark, savage face turned upwards to make him look even taller and more fearsome.

"Love!" commanded Helena, "Love, not hate! If you try to love, give instead of challenging, there's no way Genghis or his kind can win."

"I can't simply give way!" said Jason, turning towards her, but, as he did so, he saw Genghis had moved and was now in the frame next to Helena's.

"Leave her alone!" he cried, rushing forward, but the soldier simply rushed back at him, his club raised higher, roaring in delight and hatred combined. Jason hesitated a moment, trying to pull his fuddled wits together, and he turned briefly to his left. David stood sideways on to him, looking at him askance.

"Use your brain, Jason, " he said.

Jason stopped and turned the other way and realised all the other individuals were staring at him. He became conscious of the bottle he held in his hand and he was filled with disgust. He raised it above his head and hurled it at the stone fireplace where it shattered, and a thick wave of whisky fumes rose round him.

Before he knew what was happening, the spirit ignited, and the empty cartons and the easy chairs began to burn and in no time at all the room was full of flames. In the glass all round the images danced like a scene from Dante's Inferno, and Jason could hear all the voices screaming at once. He ran helplessly round as the flames surrounded him and cut him off from the windows themselves. There was no way to reach the staircase. He staggered and fled through the flames towards the sliding windows and the balcony, hitting it hard and feeling his feet slip beneath him as he fell over and tumbled, down, down to the granite on which the lighthouse stood.

Just before he landed, and the sounds of fire and wind disappeared in one final, jarring shock, he heard the voice of Genghis shouting, "Good for you, Jason the Warrior, good for you! A man after all."

The Omen

The motorbike bucked and slithered, and Peter needed all his strength and skill to keep it upright on this rough track. He was obliged to travel at walking pace and for much of the time he found he needed to use his feet to prevent the machine from falling over. It was heavily laden with two panniers which held his basic supplies. On his back the large rucksack contained his clothes and bedding so that his centre of gravity was high.

"It's very primitive and isolated," Jeremy had said. He had been right about the isolated bit: this track seemed endless at such a slow speed although Peter knew it was about a mile from the minor road to the cottage. It had been raining ever since he set out three hours earlier. On either side of the track the ground was rough, small rocks shone black in the rain. Where there was any earth to grow in, sedges and tussock grass grew. He could not look up from the track immediately in front of him.

When at last he reached the end of the track, the ground sloped steeply down in front of him for 20 or 30 yards to a rocky foreshore. All at once the rain stopped. Peter turned off the engine and looked down at the little inlet which was to be his home for the next six weeks. As he watched, the cloud which had wrapped him round for so long dispersed in a matter of minutes and weak sunlight took its place. The cottage was at the head of the inlet about 40 yards to his right. It certainly looked primitive from the outside, the walls built of the same rock as surrounded it, two small windows, a solid-looking door and a roof of slate from which water still dripped. As he took in the view a brilliant rainbow arched over the shore as though to frame the cottage. Peter hoped it was a good omen.

"I need to get completely away," he had told Jeremy. "I know I can write this book, but not here, not in London, surrounded by traffic, friends and every kind of diversion. I need no distraction. If it was practicable I would go camping, but it would be difficult to write in a tent." So, Jeremy had made his offer. Now Peter was installed.

Everything was damp. It took him nearly an hour to light a fire but, once it was burning brightly in the fireplace, the whole room changed its nature. He set about cleaning furniture and floor and he unrolled his sleeping bag in the small bedroom. He collected fresh water in the bucket he found and filled the kettle at the beck. Before nightfall he had cooked himself a meal on the open fire. Everything he needed for writing was set out on the simple table in front of the window. He had enough supplies to last at least two weeks and if he needed more, he would have to retrace his journey to the nearest village about 15 miles away. This was the isolation he wanted.

Beginning the following morning, he established a routine. It was regulated by the sun because there was no other form of lighting except for candles. He had not thought to bring oil for the lamps. His days began at sunrise and ended mostly at sunset, though he was wont to wander down to the sea after sunset just to enjoy the sense of its intensity and vastness. First thing every morning he jogged around the shoreline and collected driftwood to burn on the fire. It burned with a wonderful, blue flame. After a simple breakfast of porridge he began work and continued until he could do no more that day. Then he cooked himself something to eat. Once or twice he tried fishing but realised it was another distraction. He could stand on the rocks, rod in hand for hours, allowing himself to enjoy the sight of the sea.

Most days it seemed to rain. He did not really mind since he was less tempted to leave his workplace at the kitchen table. His writing grew steadily more productive. His only companions were gulls for the most part but on one occasion when he was gazing idly at the sea, he saw the shining backs of a pod of dolphins.

He made the difficult and uncomfortable trip to the nearest shop just once. It felt strange talking to the shop assistant, even though it was only a simple transaction. He bought oil and was thus able to light some lamps in the evening. The yellow light made the room warmer and enabled him to work on. To his delight he finished the draft in six weeks. He left the cottage with regret. He had not expected that. Rucksack once more on his back, and with a heavily laden bike, he skittered his way across the few yards to the top of the little slope where the track began. He stopped for a moment for a last look. As though on cue a rainbow formed. Peter turned onto the track and began the long ride home.

Protecting Grandad

Miss Carter, Martin's teacher, was fun. She always had lots of new ideas, some of them pretty wild, but there was no chance of being bored in her class. When Martin overheard the Headmistress one day say to a colleague, "Yes, she's full of new ideas; not all of them are good ones," he was quite distressed. Miss Carter could do no wrong.

She loved reading fantasy and was very knowledgeable about the Lord of the Rings, which explained how it was that her brain and her eyes deceived her when she began her latest interest, Persia, and the Thousand and One Nights. She seized on the story of Scheherazade as an excellent project for her class. There were all kinds of wonderful stories about Sinbad and his voyages and Miss Carter even promised she would bring in a couple of films. She talked to the children about the genie in the bottle, but she said she didn't want to use the word "genie" because she had a friend of that name, so she preferred to call the imprisoned spirit a *djinn*, which she said was a perfectly good alternative. She told them all about the wonderful, fantasy creatures, including huge birds capable of picking up elephants in their talons. They were known, she said, as Orcs, a confusion that was understandable, since Orcs occurred in Tolkien; every time she came across Rocs her eyes told her the word was Orcs, not terribly important, one would think, but a typical inaccuracy that could lead to strange consequences.

Young Martin also loved dropping in on his grandparents. They lived in a cottage at the other end of the village. His parents were busy, and although he was only seven, they were glad for him to pedal his cycle the few yards down the peaceful village lane from their spacious house, full of light, the kitchen and bathroom surfaces gleaming clinically white, to the old-fashioned cottage. The small sitting room was cosy, the chintzy armchairs soft and comfortable for a young boy to curl up in. The big chair near the fireplace was reserved for Grandad and Martin would often climb on his knee and share it. These visits were almost daily during the school holidays although Martin's mother worked from home. She spent much of her time, when not looking after the house, typing in the study she shared with her husband.

Martin timed his call mid-morning when the couple were about to have a cup of tea. He knew he would always be offered a piece of cake. Grandma was a great cake maker. He never knew what kind of cake he would be offered, nor was he sure which was his favourite; Victoria sponge, Battenburg – he thought that was cleverly made - date and walnut, occasionally a Dundee cake, full of fruit. He was not too keen on seed cake, though he ate it with interest and no obvious loss of appetite.

They were always pleased to see him. Occasionally he would find his grandmother on her own because Grandad still played golf and, being retired, he could choose a day when the course was not too busy. Martin enjoyed his grandmother's company, but it was his grandad he found more interesting. He not only had tales to tell of days of old, of travels in strange lands, but he had a wonderful and mixed collection of curios which he had collected over the years. He and his wife would occasionally wander round antique shops and from time to time they came back with a small object of little value except for its curiosity.

So, Martin was amazed and excited one day when Grandad casually mentioned watching Orcs on a trip to the north of Scotland.

"You really saw Orcs, Grandad?"

"Yes, quite a colony of them. They spend a lot of their time at sea, of course. Great Auks, they're really known as."

Martin was astonished at this news and impressed. Since they were comfortably ensconced in their armchair at the time, Grandad did not think to find a suitable illustration in one of his books, so the misunderstanding was left uncorrected.

But the most long-lasting illusion occurred soon after this. Once again the teacher's mention of the travels of Sinbad was mostly to blame. The grandparents had spent an enjoyable day in Brighton. Exploring the small shops in the Lanes, they chose to look especially at those dealing in antiques. They were not in the habit of spending a lot of money, they certainly had no need nor desire to buy furniture, but they liked to bring back some small souvenir of their days out. Martin noticed it at once. High on a shelf among other small ornaments, he spotted an earthenware bottle.

"What's that, Grandad?"

"We picked that up in Brighton," he said. "Don't ever take the cork out, though, or you'll get the full force of the old spirits right in your face."

"Spirits? What kind of spirits?"

Grandad laughed. "It's an old gin bottle," he said. "You can find them sometimes."

Martin was thunderstruck. So, the genie in the bottle or the lamp was not just a story. They really made bottles to keep *djinns* in! He was so astonished he said nothing more, but from then on, whenever he visited his grandparents, his first glance was towards the shelf. Surely it was dangerous to keep the bottle there. He could not understand why they showed so little concern. It was like having a live hand grenade on the shelf. What would happen if it got knocked off and broke?

He had to wait for the opportunity to do something about it. A week or two after his grandparents had acquired the bottle, Martin visited his grandmother. She gave him tea and a slice of carrot cake and smiled to see him tuck in.

"I've got to prepare some vegetables for dinner," she said, as she collected the cups and plates. "It'll take a minute or two. You'll be all right in here, won't you, love?"

"OK," he said, then correcting himself, "Yes, Grandma."

As soon as he was alone in the little room, he climbed on the arm of the chair, using one hand to balance himself against the bookshelves, and he reached up with the other. Carefully he grasped the bottle and lifted it down. His heart was racing. How to get it out of the cottage? He pushed the bottle up his jumper and called through to his grandma, "I think I'll go home, Grandma. See you tomorrow." Before the lady had time to dry her hands and look back into the sitting room Martin had let himself out the front door and had seized his bike. One hand clutched to his bulging jumper, he pushed his bike with the other rather than risk riding it with the dangerous cargo.

At home his mother was still in the study. She called out to him as he let himself in. But he had serious work to do. He made his way out to the garden, found a trowel in the shed, and then went to the furthest flower bed at the bottom. There he dug a hole as deeply as he could and with great care buried the bottle, making sure the cork was safe first. That done, he smoothed the soil over the spot and put the trowel back. Then he sighed with relief at a dangerous mission accomplished. He went back to the house by the kitchen door and was washing his hands at the sink when his mother came in.

"What have you been up to?" she asked.

He span round guiltily. "Nothing,"

"You've got mud all over your sweater," his

mother said. "How did that get there?"

"I fell over." It was a simple lie and it worked. He was told to change his clothes and put the dirty jersey in the wash. After that nothing more was said.

The buried bottle remained a matter of concern for Martin. He knew he had done the right thing, making sure his grandparents were no longer in danger, but he found himself making frequent visits to the flower border. Would the genie be strong enough to blow out the cork and then to explode upwards in the soil? It seemed unlikely and as days stretched into weeks he began to believe all was well. There was an awkward moment when Grandad brought up the subject of the missing bottle.

"Don't suppose you know anything about it," he said one day to Martin. "I'm sure I haven't moved the bottle since I put it on the shelf that day. Your Grandma is sure she didn't move it, but it seems to have disappeared as though by magic."

Martin didn't meet his eyes but looked at the floor and shook his head.

"Not exactly your cup of tea, eh? Not unless you've developed a sudden taste for very old spirits, that is." And he laughed. Martin did his best to laugh too, though he could not see it was funny.

Things might have remained thus for ever. Then, one crisp, dry autumn day, his parents decided to spend a few hours clearing out the old borders. With growing sense of horror Martin saw his father seize a spade and begin to plunge it vigorously into the earth, crusted over now with frost. From the kitchen window he saw the site of operations was very close to the buried treasure. He ran into the garden and down towards the flower bed just as his father dug down with huge energy in the very spot he had buried the bottle. From a few feet away, he heard the sound of breaking crockery and he shrieked out loud, expecting to see some kind of coloured cloud burst from the ground and shape itself into a monstrous, evil spirit. Nothing happened. His parents, startled by the shriek, were looking at him in astonishment. He could not speak, but pointed mutely at the spot. His father, extremely puzzled, looked at the broken soil.

"What is it, Martin?" he asked with genuine concern.

His son still found it impossible to speak, but pointed down. His father could see nothing except a couple of sherds of broken pot. He picked them up and placed them on the grass behind him, then dug more until the remains of a complete bottle lay there.

"You've let it out," Martin gasped. He was clearly distressed.

"Let what out?"

"The *djinn*. Where has it gone?"

And the story came out, Miss Carter, the Thousand and One Nights, Grandad's bottle, the need to remove the danger. Martin's parents looked and listened with growing astonishment before they explained everything carefully and slowly.

The following week they paid a visit to the school. Miss Carter laughed gaily at first but then, catching Martin's expression, she stopped.

"Oh, Martin," she said, "I'm so sorry. You should have told me about this. It was only a story. There's no such thing as a *djinn* or a genie in a bottle. You mustn't let your imagination run away with you like that."

"Perhaps," said Martin's father, "You need to remember you are dealing with imaginative children."

The following term the class began reading The Hobbit. It was a good story, Martin told his parents, but somehow it wasn't such fun this time, now he knew it wasn't real.

First Impressions

At the age of 22 Chris Watkins considered himself lucky. It was indeed a matter of
luck that he had been born with an innate aptitude for mathematics. In his teens he realised that if he were to pursue his interest, it would involve hard work and dedication as well as enjoyment. He had risen to the challenge, and his diligence had taken him to this point, one year short of his PhD. Then fate stepped in. He met Meredith.

His relationships with women had always been intentionally superficial. He had no wish to get emotionally involved until he had completed his doctorate. He was happy to meet girls and to chat and enjoy their company but as soon as he recognised the stirrings of lust, for his intelligence extended beyond his mathematical prowess, he disciplined himself to walk away. It was preferable to take a cold shower. Until he met Meredith, that is.

Meredith, ("call me Mary"), was petite, vibrantly alive, always cheerful and for reasons that were inexplicable as attracted to Chris as he was to her. After the initial meeting at a small party thrown by mutual friends Chris was dismayed to find his attention wandering and progress on his research slowing. He redoubled his efforts to no avail. He tried to forget the girl, but her image continually swam into his memory, her laughter rang in his ears, and fragments of conversation came back unbidden. "I didn't quite know what to do after graduation. I wasn't good enough to make a living as a musician. When my mother died, my father insisted on giving me the insurance. It was enough to set up a little music shop. Merry and bright, that's me."

Attempts to ignore the distraction proved a failure and with the kind of helplessness Chris took the opposite direction and pursued the object of his desire. For a while the intense pleasure almost masked the guilt he felt at neglecting his work but the situation could not continue in this way. They moved in together. It worked well. Merry was out all day and occasionally she was out in the evenings too. Chris had the flat to himself knowing that Merry would be back all in good time.

"I've had an email from Daddy," she announced one morning. "He's coming to town next Tuesday to see his publisher in the morning, but he says he'd like to come to see us both. I shan't be able to get away before 6 o'clock. You won't mind entertaining him for the afternoon, will you?"

"I – er – no, I suppose not." Chris was taken aback. "You've not said very much about your father. I don't even know what he does for a living."

"He's a writer. He makes a living from his main interest in life. He and Mummy were both great naturalists. If you want to get on his good side, just show a real interest, pretend if you like."

Nervously Chris agreed. He knew that he

would be unable to concentrate on work on Tuesday morning, so he spent a few hours on domestic chores. He was in the habit of looking after the flat himself. As the expected visit approached – Sir Lionel (Chris was doubly uncertain about entertaining a knight of the realm who was also a naturalist) – his nervousness grew. He tried to concentrate on Merry's advice, wondering how he was to show any kind of interest in Sir Lionel's affairs.

At 3 o'clock the doorbell rang. Chris took a quick look through the peephole and saw a bearded man with a suntanned face. He opened the door and said, his voice breaking with nervousness, "Sir Lionel, please come in, I'm Chris."

'"Good God!" Sir Lionel stared at the young man. "You knew I was coming; did you not have time to get dressed?"

Chris stared at his nakedness with great embarrassment. "Merry said you were a naturalist and I should try to make you feel at home…"

The astonishment on Sir Lionel's face changed slowly and then all at once gave way to a kind of delight followed by uncontrollable mirth. He laughed until he cried, and he was still laughing when Chris returned from the bedroom, wearing a T-shirt and jeans and a look of total humiliation. The older man slapped Chris on the back and shook his hand.

"I'm not a *naturist*," he said, "I'm *a naturalist*. I don't prance around in the nude: I study nature and write articles about it. Now, young man, have you got anything to drink?"

Merry came home at about 6:30 to find the two men busy in the kitchen preparing dinner. They were clearly getting on well. She ran to her father and gave him a big hug. "Chris wasn't meant to set you to work," she said.

"I volunteered."

"What do you think of him, Daddy?"

"Very open," he said solemnly. "Refreshingly naive, perhaps, but I think I've had more than a glimpse of what it is that attracts you to him."

Inquisition

He had no idea how he got into this room. He was aware only that he was sitting at a table on the other side of which there were a man and a woman, strangers. The man was dressed in a grey suit and it was impossible to guess his age. The woman, also in a suit, wore no make-up, was possibly in her forties, unsmiling.

'Wht is this?' Jack asked. 'Where am I? Who are you?'

'We ask the questions. You simply answer them.'

'Am I accused of something?'

'Not exactly. Why? Have you something you want to tell us about?'

'I demand to know what this is about. Do I need a solicitor?'

'You are not permitted a solicitor,' the man replied firmly.

'Then I shall refuse to answer any questions,' said Jack, sitting back in his chair with the air of a card player who has played his key trump.

'Your silence will be taken as evidence of your concurring with our own observations in that case.'

'That is outrageous!'

The inquisitor nodded. 'That is the usual reaction,' he said. 'But first let me explain that this interview will be recorded. It will also be observed through that two-way mirror you can see over there. We already have a full dossier pertaining to you.'

Jack began to sweat a little.

'Your full name is Jack Randolph Partrige.' The woman spoke this time in an expressionless voice. It was a statement, not a question. 'You were born in 1950 in Horsham, West Sussex. You worked as a clerk in the offices of Balcombe and Sons for five years while studying in your own time to qualify in accountancy.'

It was all true.

'Subsequently,' the woman continued, 'You were self-employed and very successful. Among your clients were a Thomas Cropper and a Felicity Martin.'

At the names, Jack stiffened. He had not thought of them for years but had deliberately pushed them into the darkest recesses of his forgetfulness. They had been the secrets of his success financially; they were both elderly clients whose money he had quite simply embezzled and invested on his own account to make a small fortune in each case. They had not suspected anything and each of them in turn had died before there was a chance of his crime coming to light. He had covered his tracks well. How, he wondered, had these people, whoever they were, discovered the information. Wasn't there in any case a statute of limitation, because these events had taken place at least thirty years ago. Since then he had prospered legitimately. No one, he told himself, had been seriously hurt by his activities except for the heirs of the two clients, who suspected nothing. Since the same heirs had not expected to inherit anything much in the first case, they had not been disappointed when the legacies proved very small.

'We are fully aware of your fraudulent activities with respect to Mr Cropper and Mrs Martin,' the man said. 'Are you prepared to admit to your crimes, and have you anything to say as a form of contrition?'

Contrition! What a strange word to choose, thought Jack, but he maintained the same silence.

'If you do not answer, I would remind you we take it as proof of guilt. What happens next is not up to us.'

'Then I want to speak directly to your superior.'

'That is not possible. No one is allowed to see him face to face.'

They waited for a few minutes before the woman switched off the recorder and they both stood up. Jack did likewise, glancing down at the table for the first time to see a folder. His own name caught his eye and he managed to read the label before the inquisitors picked up the papers. Each gave a little resigned sigh and turned to leave the room, glancing up at the two-way mirror with what looked like an apologetic shrug.

The title on the file read, 'Jack Randolph Partridge' but what made him react with an immense sense of dismay were the numbers that followed: 1950 – 2015.

Charlie the clown.

Sarah was exhausted. It was approaching the end of her Friday night shift in A and E. Friday nights were always bad. As usual there had been high incidence of alcohol fuelled problems. She had seen so many of them that she lacked any kind of sympathy for the victims although she continued to treat their cuts and bruises or even on occasion fractures as professionally as ever. They had been obliged to call the police to remove to aggressive males, one of whom had managed to knock out Poor Colin, the triage nurse.

She had just washed her hands when the next patient was ushered in. Once more Sarah found it hard, when she looked at him not to be annoyed. He was dressed as a clown. His face was covered in grease paint except for his nose where he had presumably worn a red button nose. Too large, false tears were painted on his cheeks. The big, silky shirt with flowing sleeves, the extravagantly large tie and the now very badly soiled rough round his neck simply made her even more annoyed. He was wearing ordinary shoes, not the absolutely huge slippers she associated with this kind of dress. The volume and as trousers were badly torn and there appeared to be quite a lot of blood on one leg.

"I suppose this was a stag party?" she asked.

"No, nothing like that!" His voice was vaguely familiar.

"I can't deal with you when you're wearing a mask," she said impatiently, and handed him a pot of cream and a handful of paper towels. Obediently he rubbed the copious quantity over his painted face and wiped it clean with the towels. Sarah held open the bin for him to throw them in.

"The wound appears to be at the back," she said. "Take off those silly trousers and lie down on that count for me on your stomach."

It seemed to be a painful business for him, the clothing had stuck to the wound. Still impatient, Sarah stepped forward, pulled down the garment for him.

Unlike the knife wounds which she had treated earlier that evening, this one was far less clean, and different in kind. "This looks like an animal bite," she said. "How did this happen?"

"It was my dog, Brutus."

"Your own dog? Judging by the size of the bite he must be a big animal." She was busy cleaning the wound as best she could, but it was untidy, and she had to use tweezers to remove pieces of cloth which had been forced in by the dog's teeth. "Is he in the habit of biting people like this?"

"No, never... Ouch!" Sarah apologised. The man continued, "I have no idea what made him do it. He is the most reliable of all my dogs."

"How many do you have?"

"I use four for my act"

"Your act?"

"I work in the circus. I thought that was obvious."

"Tell me more. This is going to take a few minutes and it will take your mind off things until I've cleaned up the wound. You're not going to want to sit down much for a week or two."

"Well," the clown explained, "it's a straightforward clown act, the sort you see in lots of circuses. You know the sort of thing: I say things like, "This dog is very intelligent: it can even pick out famous composers from their pictures," then I bring out three big paintings and I get a dog to look at the first one and I say, "Who's this?" And the dog goes woof and I say, of course, it's Bach. Then I pointed at the next painting and he goes woof, woof, woof, and I say loudly, "Well done! It's Offenbach, but I bet you can't tell me who the third one is." Then the dog shakes his head bit as though he's puzzled before he runs out of the ring and there is kind of shriek before he comes back with a pair of stays in his teeth. I say, "yes, you're right, it's Ripsmecorsetsoff."

"But how did he come to bite you?"

"Well, that's the end of the act, when I stand at the edge of the ring and tell the audience what clever animals they are and how the whole act is based on mutual trust and as I take my final bow Brutus runs forward and pretends to bite me on the bum. But this time he did it in earnest."

Sarah finished disinfecting the wound and put in three stitches, telling him he would have to come back in a week's time to have them removed. She asked the nurse to find a suitable pair of trousers for the patient. Then she said, "There's something familiar about you, your voice. Have we met before?"

"My name is Charlie Mellow."

"Good heavens!" We were at school together many years ago. My name is Sarah Haggerty.

The encounter had lifted her mood and, as she climbed wearily into her car with a smile on her face, she thought she might visit the circus on her day off, even if there were no dogs.

Brief Encounter

For some reason the train was packed as far as Taunton that night. My first class seat was reserved. The young woman who asked, "Is this seat free?" was astonishingly beautiful. She was blonde, her hair tidy as only an expensive hairdresser could make it. The features were regular, the eyes large, clear, blue, and the mouth sensuous with the slightest trace of a smile to indicate good humour. She wore an expensive suit which emphasised her curves to perfection yet allowed her to move in comfort like a cat, athletic yet graceful. She sat down next to me.

Half an hour out of Reading the train slowed and stopped. The train manager told us over the crackly loudspeaker that there was a problem with the signals. Soon the carriage was full of loud voices as the passengers relayed the information by their mobile phones to waiting husbands, wives, partners and colleagues. I did not follow suit. Experience had taught me that the delay might well be longer, possibly shorter before the train arrived in Truro.

We were on the move again in ten minutes but at walking speed. The driver, we were told, had to inspect the line ahead for the next twenty miles because there was a report of cows on the line. This brought a smile to my lips and to those of my neighbour.

"That's a new one," I remarked.

"Not so worrying as children on the line," she replied. "Do you often travel this way?"

And so the conversation began, a little intermittent to begin with until we reached Taunton. After that, in the less crowded carriage, we chatted more. Her name was Helen and she was travelling to Newton Abbot to visit her parents. They had retired to Devon several years ago, but she worked in London. She loved Devon, but her work kept her far too busy to get home more than once or twice a year. I asked what she did.

"I'm in public relations," she said.

I didn't like to push it further; 'public relations' was such a general phrase it might apply to anything, but we were strangers. To ask too many questions would make me sound like a detective.

"I'd hate to work in London," I confided. "I was born and bred in the country and I still love it in spite of all its disadvantages. It might be great to be able to go to concerts and the theatre whenever you wish, but I love the sea and the sky and the wide open spaces."

She smiled. "True," she said, "But needs must when the devil drives."

"I haven't heard that expression for years."

The conversation developed and all at once I found I was talking about myself because Helen had a knack which I only recognised in hindsight; she was able to make me feel relaxed and strangely important. She seemed genuinely interested in me, those lovely eyes sparkling and teeth flashing as she spoke to me. For my part, though I longed to know more about her as an individual, I was unsure how to ask without being intrusive.

The time passed very quickly, and we reached Exeter St Davids. As we pulled out towards the finest views of the coast past Dawlish and Teignmouth, the train manager came to check our tickets. I had mine ready and handed it over just as Helen was opening her handbag. In so doing I knocked her bag clumsily, spilling some of its contents on the table in front of us, bits fell to the floor. I apologised and began to help pick it all up.

"Don't worry," she said. "Leave it to me. No harm done."

But I was embarrassed by my clumsiness and continued to help. Afterwards we lapsed into silence for a while and, after passing Teignmouth it seemed no time at all before we were coming into Newton Abbot. Helen smiled as she prepared to leave, said it had been nice to meet me, and made her way to the door.

Her departure left me alone with nearly two hours to my destination. The buffet closed as usual at Totnes, re-opening at Liskeard, where I made my way there to buy a cup of coffee. I lurched back to my seat with the little paper bag in one hand and set it on the table in order to pour out the drink. I dropped one of the little packets of sugar which fell on the seat. I leaned sideways to pick it up and noticed a small piece of card which had become lodged in the crack between the two seats. I pulled it out.

It looked very much like a business card. It was the right size and shape. I turned it over to read the name.

>
> CARMEN LITTLE
> Totally discreet personal massage service etc.
> 0739 6241 3177
>

It was the 'etc' which made me gulp, that and the realisation that 'public relations' might have a specific meaning after all.

Bless you – a life story.

Johnnie was a bonny baby. Everyone said so. His proud parents positively glowed with pride. He left the hospital with his mother, Muriel, three days after the birth. Frank, his father, carried the child in its little basket to the car and handed him to Muriel when she was settled in the back seat. They were both smiling broadly as they drove home.

For the first two weeks all went well. There was the usual panic as the new parents dealt with this fragile bundle of flesh and blood. They were as prepared as most for the messier bits, changing nappies was the least attractive chore, but Muriel found feeding the child more difficult than she had expected. Nevertheless, they managed well enough. Frank's mother cooed over her grandchild and tried not to interfere but did so anyway. Muriel's mother, who had come to stay 'just to help you out for a week or two', interfered rather more in a kindly way until, after the first two weeks, her daughter suggested she needed to learn to cope on her own. Hiding her resentment, she duly left. Frank's mother still visited at least twice a week, but she was, as Muriel told her husband, 'more manageable'.

In the third week the two parents had the baby to themselves. It was half way through the week that Johnnie sneezed for the first time. Now, whenever a small baby sneezes it comes as a surprise not only to the child itself but also to anyone nearby. On this occasion it was more than a simple surprise which would make them laugh. The noise was more like an explosion. Johnnie was lying in his carry cot which was on the sofa. The sneeze was so forceful that the sofa actually bounced, tiny splashes of saliva were thrown across the room, some even ending up on the window in the opposite wall. Inevitably, too, Johnnie filled his nappy suddenly and copiously. Muriel was the only witness to this phenomenon, the suddenness of which made her jump and then laugh. She set about cleaning up the aftermath. The baby was otherwise in fine fettle. That evening Muriel told her husband about the unexpected event and he, too, laughed.

Frank bore the full brunt of the next infant sneeze. He was truly astonished by its force. With good humour he set about tidying up the results, laughed out loud, talked engagingly to his son, later told his wife about it. What neither of them could know was that this was to be a regular feature of Johnnie's life. As he grew, so did his sneezing. There was nothing regular or predictable about it; there was no obvious cause; the house was as clean and dust-free as an anxious mother and two concerned grandmothers could make it; there were no draughts anyone could find. Changing the washing powder for the baby's clothes and for the bedclothes made no difference. From time to time Johnnie sneezed with growing and worrying violence. Still, unpredictable it might be, but it was relatively harmless, a cause for amusement rather than concern. Once potty training had been completed, too, the after-effects of one of Johnnie's attacks were rather less insanitary, although some warning and the use of a handkerchief would have been a distinct advantage.

At three and a half Muriel took him to a nursery for the first time. He loved mixing with the other children and got on well, At least he got on well for the first two weeks, then one morning he was engaged in building a tall tower of plastic bricks together with four others and one of the adults when he sneezed. The bricks flew in all directions, the young woman was taken totally by surprise, and the other children were shocked and then began to cry, all of them at once. It took the supervising staff over half an hour to calm them down and they then had the unenviable task of cleaning the children, the bricks and other equipment and wiping down the floor and other surfaces with one of the solvents that killed all known germs.

The manager of the nursery interrogated Muriel. "Is Johnnie coming down with a cold?" she asked.

"No. He does this from time to time," his mother explained. "It's always without warning."

"Well, it caused chaos this morning."

Muriel apologised and felt unfairly embarrassed. At home she made an appointment with her GP.

The doctor examined the toddler and declared him healthy. He suggested some minor allergy might be the cause, but he felt that to conduct a full test for allergies might be going too far. After all Johnnie was only three years old and the only problem was that he had a propensity to sneeze. True it was unexpectedly at times, but surely it was harmless. He had no communicable diseases to spread.

Muriel reported this consultation to the lady in charge of the nursery who appeared satisfied and Johnnie was welcomed back, albeit with some reserve on the part of the adult staff. A week later, however, another sneeze proved disruptive in the extreme; at one end of the room, fenced off from the children's play area, was the kitchen and one of the young women was busy makng tea when the explosion occurred. The suddenness and above all the loudness so startled her that she dropped the jug of boiling water, scalding both feet and one arm. She screamed at the shock and the ensuing chaos meant that she was taken off to hospital, leaving the nursery short-staffed and compelling the manager to close it for two days.

Johnnie was banned. His father was more than indignant; "I think we should sue them," he said. "How can they blame a small child like this? They are supposed to be professionals and should surely be prepared to deal with anything small children can do."

But they took no action and readjusted their plans. Muriel gave up any hope of returning to work for a year or two, but maybe, once Johnnie joined a Junior School, she would be free to think about it.

Further incidents were to occur throughout junior school days. After the first two occasions the

Headteacher remarked in a tone which suggested she cared about the child (when in fact it was more a matter of enlightened self-interest) that Johnnie's parents should ask for further medical advice. The sneezing was so violent and unpredictable there must surely be some underlying cause. And so began a long series of consultations, a full allergy test in which a series of pinpricks were left on the child's arm and tine samples of possible allergens were dropped on the wounds. There was no reaction. Muriel was asked to keep detailed notes for two months of everything Johnnie ate, his bowel movements, the clothes he wore, the environments in which he was exposed to possible chemical contaminents and even some personal questions about stress within the marriage and relationships between parents and child. None of this revealed anything of interest.

In desperation the baffled consultants arranged a magnetic resonance scan. It, too, was negative. They remained baffled, but Johnnie still sneezed unpredictably and with increasing violence.

This strange condition proved a continuing source of anxiety to his parents. Now they found themselves on edge all the time, waiting for the inevitable loud noise. They began to argue about the future , arguments which blighted their relationship for years until Johnnie left home many years later. It was not the happiest home environment.

So much medical attention had been lavished ineffectually on Johnnie that it was impossible not to mention it when he was seeking admission to a secondary school Within four weeks of joining the local comprehensive his mother was called in to see the Headmaster.

"I realise you told us about Johnnie's – er – condition when he was enrolled," he said, "But we really had no understanding of the likely consequences."

"It hasn't affected his growth nor his intelligence," said Muriel.

"I meant the consequences for his classmates," he explained. "At first they found the sneezing funny, but then there was the occasion in the woodwork shop…"

"I am very sorry about that," said Muriel. "How is young Jason?"

"Recovering. I hope you understand that we cannot take chances like this in the future. I'm afraid I shall have to limit the activities Johnnie can take part in. Any activity where a sudden or unexpected noise is likely to cause disruption will be out, I'm afraid."

"Which activities are you talking about?"

"Obviously any which involve the use of sharp implements – woodwork, metalwork, many games activities – imagine the damage that a misplaced javelin could cause, or, for that matter, a faulty approach to someone on a vaulting horse or climbing a rope. The list will be quite long, I'm afraid."

Muriel was forced to accept such terms, but Johnnie's secondary education was limited. For similar reasons he never learned to ride a bicycle and later driving was out of the question. His life was severely compromised.

What took longer to sink in was the more subtle effect on his social life because he found it very hard to make and maintain friendships. The unpredictability of his attacks was their worst feature and he began to develop a constant, nagging anxiety. It left him less able to enjoy life spontaneously. He was particularly reluctant to form any kind of romantic relationship until he met Belinda, known variously as Belle or Linda, depending on the status of the friend. Johnnie called her Linda. He was strongly drawn to her when they met at a local jazz club. Johnnie found that the music was generally so loud and marked by powerful drumming that a sneeze, though it would still be audible, would be less of a shock to the ears of those present. After one evening at the club he spoke to Linda outside and romance blossomed. At first the meetings were brief and casual but one evening Johnnie took his courage in his hands and asked Linda out for a meal.

The restaurant was a pleasant one and relatively expensive because he was keen to impress. He gazed at this lovely girl across the table and his heart was thumping. Was this, he wondered, what falling in love was like. The first course arrived, a creamy, tomato soup on which floated a circle of herbs and steam rose appealingly. They began to eat, finding it difficult to wrench their eyes from one another's face to glance down at the soup itself.

Then Johnnie sneezed.

Although an attack came with no warning whatsoever, each sneeze required him first to take in a very deep breath. The sound of this great gasp was enough to make Linda look up in surprise, so she was facing Johnnie full on when the sneeze came. All the soup was blown in a great, red spray, bouncing off the inward curve of the bowl so that it spread far and wide, but much of it was hurled like a furious squall into Linda's face. Both Johnnie and Linda were smothered in soup, the immaculate table linen was ruined, a passing waiter caught much of the blast, but there was sufficient left of the energy dispensed to splash at least twelve other customers who had the misfortune to be seated nearby.

After that Johnnie's embarrassment was enough to end the relationship before it had properly begun, and he stopped attending the jazz club.

He sought treatment from a hypnotist. Believing it had solved his problem, or at least hoping it had. Johnnie lost some of his customary sense of anxiety, but he was not entirely sure the treatment would be successful after twenty years or more. He decided his only course of action was to find a way of life which was solitary, preferably in wild places where he would not disturb others. He needed a job he could do alone. He thought about it long and hard. To help him decide he saved some money and set off on a long walk in the wildest place he know of,

Yellowstone National Park.

He prepared meticulously, walking long distances to get fit. He bought the best equipment he could afford without overloading his backpack. And so he found himself one fine spring morning, striding happily along the trail. He walked for three days and met only two people. He camped out each night, drank water from the clear streams, enjoyed the immensity of the park as he climbed into the hills through stands of great trees. From time to time he stopped and spent half an hour at a time simply gazing with his binoculars at the wildlife, particularly the birds, which fascinated him. He was exhilarated. He kept detailed notes of all the wildlife he saw. This, he felt more and more sure, was the future for him. Whatever it took, he would train to be a ranger in some such environment.

The fourth night he pitched his tent in a clearing close to the trees. The view was wonderful, and he enjoyed it as he ate his dinner, which he prepared on a small camp fire. Dusk fell. The sunset was bewitching and he sat outside his tent gazing at the spectacle of the sky, as the colours faded and deepened.

Suddenly he was aware of movement behind him and to his left. He turned and saw a large bear, attracted by the smell of his cooking, no doubt. It approached on all fours but, less than twenty feet from him it reared on its hind legs. It must be at least eight feet tall, he thought in alarm, as it began to waddle towards him and a good meal.

Then he sneezed.

The bear was not merely astonished, it was terrified. It wheeled round, dropped back to all fours and ran off as quickly as possible into the timber.

It was this experience which settled Johnnie's future. For the first time ever his sneezing had not had a negative outcome and he felt for once a little more confident in himself. From now on he would work in the wilderness, how or where he would decide in due course.

It took him two more years to find the answer. He teamed up with a small trader who worked out of the north of Canada, travelling to remote Inuit villages. After a while he felt competent to set up independently. He did well, spending much of his time recording, photographing and writing about the wildlife on or near the Arctic Circle and eking out a living by trading.

He settled in a small village where he bought a redundant trading store which had been established by the Hudson Bay Trading Company. It was on one side of a headland and another settlement lay on the other side, accessible only by dog sled over a hazardous route overlooking the Bay. Johnnie's opening day in his new store was memorable. About a dozen curious villagers crowded in, eager to see what goods he had to offer. It was warm inside from a gas heater. The supply ship brought in large gas cylinders on its annual visits.

As the customers browsed, Johnnie sneezed.

For several seconds there was a shocked silence, broken only by the jangling of pots and pans hanging on the walls and the loud barking of dogs whose owners had left them with their sleds outside. Then the customers exploded into laughter, whooping with joy and mirth. They clutched their sides, hugged one another, gasped for breath and the shack was filled with their happy noise. For once Johnnie's affliction had been interpreted as funny rather than frightening. He found himself laughing too.

From that time Johnnie was accepted, albeit with the slight reserve which is normal for a foreigner. He did not make a lot of money, but he survived financially and was free to pursue his interest in wildlife and photography. One day a customer from, the other side of the headland decided he wanted to buy a gas cooker. The problem was how to transport it together with the cylinders. Johnnie spoke to his neighbour, an Inuit he knew as Sam.

'No problem," said. Sam "If this man brings his own dog team, he can take the cooker. You pay me to take the gas.'

So, it was arranged. Johnnie would have to go with Sam and the gas in order to explain how to connect it. The customer arrived on time, his dogs' breath making white clouds in the cold air. They loaded the cooker on his sled and lashed it down. Sam turned up and to Johnnie's surprise he had brought his son, a small boy of about six. There would be three of them to accompany the gas cylinders. All was safely stowed away, and the two teams set off up the hill, the men helping by pushing the sleds. The dogs were fit and eager and Johnnie found the trip thoroughly exhilarating. It was all done in a matter of hours and the single sled with its three passengers began the return, climbing back to the top of the headland. At the top they paused briefly. Johnnie and the small boy climbed on the now empty sled.

Johnnie sneezed. The dogs were startled in the silent whiteness by this sudden blast of sound and Sam lost control. The sled skittered sideways down the slope, away from the track, careering wildly towards the steep, ice-covered cliff beyond which the land fell sharply down to the frozen Bay, many hundreds of feet below. One runner hit an obstacle of some kind and Johnnie and the child were thrown onto the snow. They slid towards the edge and dropped over. It all happened in a matter of seconds.

Johnnie found himself flat on his back on a wide ledge. Above him the snow formed a vertical wall. To his left, when he turned his head, he saw the boy, apparently unharmed, getting to his feet. In his parka he looked like a ball of cloth. And beyond the boy there was a small cave in the ice. Johnnie sat up and got to his feet. He turned to go to the child but at that point he sensed something else; on the edge of the ledge: a polar bear was also getting to its feet, about to walk towards the two humans.

Remarkably Johnnie sneezed again.

He had never sneezed twice in close

succession before. It was to save his life and that of the child, just as it had so many years previously when the bear had been a different colour. The polar bear reacted with astonishment, stepped backwards three paces and lost its footing to topple down the cliff below.

Above there was a shout. Sam lay flat on the edge or the cliff, gazing down. He retrieved his team, and threw down a rope for Johnnie. He hauled his son to safety first, then Johnnie followed. With great care they resumed their journey.

The adventure turned Johnnie into a local hero, the man who had saved Sam's son from the bear. It also convinced him that his sneezes were not necessarily a curse after all. He lived out his days in the same little community. After a couple more years he even found a wife who, like the rest of the villagers, found his affliction a matter of amusement and possibly a gift from God.

He died at the age of 76. He left a request that a simple headstone be erected over his grave and it is still there for visitors to see; beneath the name the inscription reads, "A life not to be sneezed at." The man who carved the words thought them very strange, but, after all, he had been paid for the job.

Resting

On this occasion the arrangements were unusually hurried. The owners had barely time to say hello, show me where the dogs' food was kept and to check that I could set the alarm correctly. Then with a brief handshake they were off, the Bentley's wheels crunching on the gravel

    I gazed around the sitting room with interest. I always got great enjoyment from this taking over of a luxurious house or flat for a week or two. It suited my life style. All the time the play ran six nights a week plus matinees I was too busy even to notice the frugality of the theatrical digs. Faced with a month's rest before I headed off for my summer season in Torquay, four weeks' luxury living, rent free, was very welcome. All the same it had been arranged so quickly this time that I felt mildly uncomfortable, almost apprehensive.

    My rucksack was still in the tiled hallway together with my small grip. I left them there and headed across the vastness of the sitting room to the kitchen area. There was a fancy coffee machine which would probably take me a couple of hours to master. There was nothing else on show on the granite worktops except for a flower arrangement, placed with great care. Above and below the working surface there were rows of uniform, shiny black doors. I needed a cup of tea so, unmethodically, I made a random search. I found instant coffee and sugar and behind one of the doors I found a fridge with milk. Not too far away I found an electric kettle and in one of the top cupboards some mugs.

The two German shepherds watched with half-hearted interest; Tristan and Iseult, easy names to remember. They lay, heads on paws, and watched. I looked forward to taking them for walks both in the spacious grounds and later for longer expeditions on the Downs. The fresh air and exercise seemed wonderfully attractive.

I finished my coffee and headed up the wide staircase to choose a room to sleep in. I never used the master bedrooms and there was a wide choice here. The first three all looked fine so I opted for the second of these simply because the view from the window was marginally better. As far as I could tell, when I got round to looking at about six other bedrooms, they all had en suite bathrooms.

I was just crossing the landing when I heard the click of the front door closing. I hurried down the staircase in time to see a slim, dark-haired figure enter the sitting room. I hurried after her and found her standing in the middle, fondling the dogs' ears. They clearly knew her well.

"You must be the house sitter," she said, turning to meet me.

"You have me at a disadvantage," I said. "You are..?"

"Bella. Bella Dulac."

"So Mr Dulac is your.."

"My father, yes."

"I don't understand," I said. "Why hire a house sitter like me if you live here?"

"Oh, I don't live here," she explained quickly. "I couldn't. I never come here when my parents are in residence." There was something about the emphasis she placed on "my parents" which sounded odd and there was a strangely mocking expression on her face.

"I see," I said, though I didn't. "Can I offer you a drink of tea or coffee or something?"

She was amused at that for some reason and her smile broadened as I renewed my hunting behind all the black doors. It was an attractive smile. I was beginning to like the girl. She went to one of the doors, opened it and took out a selection of coffees for the machine. She continued to smile as she showed me how to work this monstrous contraption. We sat with the results, facing one another on a pair of the leather sofas, while the dogs settled happily at Bella's feet. We talked.

The only thing she had against her father was his choice of wife. He had divorced Bella's mother when Bella was only ten years old. When he remarried five years later, it was to a highly successful interior designer. She was wealthy and spent much of her time on charitable activities. Martin Dulac was also a successful businessman, but he found himself drawn more and more by his new wife into a world of dinner parties, charity balls and fund raising. There was less and less time left for his daughter. By the time she was eighteen she had had enough and left home for good. Forced in effect to choose, her father had chosen his wife.

It was a sad story in its way. I felt sorry for the girl, so when she explained she wanted to spend a little time in what had once been her own room and that she wanted to pick out a couple of mementos to take away with her, I watched her make her way upstairs.

It was nearly an hour later that she returned with a teddy bear and a small box of oddments. She looked a little red, as though she had been crying. I said nothing. She thanked me and left, after one more pat of the dogs.

I was in Torquay five weeks later when I received the letter from Mr Dulac's solicitors. They demanded £3,500 compensation for the damage done to Mrs Dulac's wardrobe. Her designer dresses for which I was legally responsible during my stay had apparently been systematically cut to pieces by scissors. Fortunately, she had taken her jewellery with her on holiday. As well as demanding a cash settlement, the letter informed me that a copy had already been sent to the agency through which I found houses to look after. If the money was not forthcoming within one month, they would sue.

My solicitors are still working on it.

Arkwright

"God," said Noah, "I don't want to be disrespectful, but have you thought this thing through?"
He was squatting in the dust, staring at the drawings he had made.

"There you go again," God replied. It was clear from his tone that he was making a conscious effort to be patient. "I gave you a job to do and expect you to get on with it. Instead, you have to make matters complicated and you always seem to be complaining these days. You are beginning to sound like an old man."

"I turned 501 this year," Noah reminded him. "At this rate I won't get the job done before I'm 600."

God's sighed. "Very well," he said, "What's the problem now?"

"In the first place," said Noah, "You gave me all the measurements in cubits. I never did understand those, and I had to change them all into good old-fashioned feet and inches. The instructions were to build an ark, 450 feet long, 75 feet wide and 45 feet high." He paused but there was no comment. "You told me to make it with three decks and to divide it into a series of compartments and to put a door in the side. You then told me that me and my sons had to collect pairs of every kind of animal on earth as well as collecting all the necessary timbers to build the boat. All of that is going to take a long time."

"Yes, yes, yes," the Almighty was growing impatient; Noah could hear the muttering of thunder. "What's your point? Get on with it!"

"You said," Noah continued stubbornly, "That Shem, Ham and Japheth, together with their wives and me and Mrs Noah should also have accommodation on board." He paused but there was still nothing but the slight rumbling of thunder. "There simply won't be enough room for all the animals in such a small boat, especially if we are supposed to take food for them as well. There are four married couples in the family, so we will need four cabins to sleep in as well as at least one modest sized cabin where we can break bread together. And that's another thing – we'll need provisions for ourselves as well as some kind of galley for the women to do the cooking."

God gave vent to an exasperated roar. "You can't expect me to work miracles," he cried. "Use your initiative."

But Noah would not be put off. "Accommodation problems aside," he said, "There is a far bigger problem which you seem to have overlooked completely."

This time there was an angry flash of lightning as well as a deafening clap of thunder.

"Half the animals are herbivores," Noah insisted, his chin thrust out as he pressed the point home. "But the other half are carnivores who will want to eat them or, failing that, eat each other. That would defeat the object of the game, wouldn't it?"

This time there was no immediate response. After a while God said, "This is decidedly awkward. The trouble is my Word is the Law and there is no easy option. What would people think of me in future if they knew I had broken my Word?"

"What we have," said Noah at length, "Is an insoluble problem." He stood up and stared fixedly into the distance for no reason other than the belief that staring into the distance would inspire him.

"Very well," he said at last, "How's this for an idea? We let the records show that everything is done exactly as you have ordered but you leave me to work out all the details. You have to admit, God, you are best at making large-scale plans but in this case it might be best to delegate and leave me, a simple, practical man, to see to the details. That way I shall see to it that a male and female of each species survives the flood as well as the eight of us in my family."

"I suppose I don't have much choice," said God. "The important thing is the outcome and that is what I want everyone to remember in future. This will be a one-off. If you make plans like all those drawings scattered around your feet, make sure they are all destroyed so that your descendants only remember the general scheme of things. I don't want them looking back at you and your boys as role models and cultivating sinful pride because of your success in carrying out my plan."

And so it was that Noah, boatbuilder extraordinaire, took upon himself the task of designing not one ark but a small fleet. He had no idea how long the flood would last nor when it would begin. He could do no more than hope and pray that he could complete the work of building in good time. In fact, it was going to take him over 90 years to complete the build and to collect all the animals. He was thankful that he need not worry about fish or sea mammals, though he realised birds would have to be housed, since there would be no roosts for them nor food. He grumbled a little at that.

His biggest problem was how to feed the meat eaters. He housed them in their own ark, thus avoiding the danger of their predating on the herbivores. There was a distinct danger that they might eat one another, however, so he had to improvise. The third ark was full of mostly small creatures like rabbits and voles that would serve as food for the carnivores. Fortunately, many of these bred rapidly, ensuring a continual supply of live sustenance for the carnivores in Ark 2. He was a little concerned that at the end of the flood itself he might have preserved too many of these small creatures instead of just two of each kind, but then he realized that if he were to release them first, give them a head start, the predators from Ark 2 would set off in hot pursuit and thus allowed time to disembark the herbivores.

The more he thought about it and developed these plans, the more sophisticated they became. He gave up worrying about the passage of time and hardly even noticed he was approaching his 600th birthday. By then he had increased the fleet to include yet another ark. He had realized quite early on that the accommodation for the herbivores was very squashed. When his sons returned from one expedition in Africa with male and female specimens of rhinoceros, hippopotamus and elephant, he knew his misgivings had been well founded. When it became apparent that the elephant alone would eat vast quantities of hay on a daily basis, it was obvious one Ark could not possibly contain both animals and fodder.

On his 600th birthday therefore Noah sat in the middle of a very large zoological park. Hundreds of animals were held in pens and cages ready for embarkation, and the family had their work cut out to ensure they were all fed at regular intervals – some, like the big cats, need only be fed every third day, but some of the herbivores seemed to eat continuously.

The family celebrated his 600th birthday with a barbecue. For once it was the younger men, Noah's sons, who were responsible for the cooking while the old man sat back in his chair and gazed with satisfaction at the four enormous boats. He took a drink of his favourite wine and gazed benignly at his family. The sun was setting, and the smell of roasting food reminded him just how hungry he was. He looked up at the sky above and blinked: the stars disappeared behind a screen of cloud from which he could feel the first splashes of rain. There was a sudden squall that put out the fires. Noah heard in the stirring of the dust and the swirling of the wind the voice of God, "I, your God, am a jealous God."

He groaned. "You might have let me have my birthday in peace," he said.

The flood came quickly and kept them all even busier than they had been for the previous 90 years or more. The foodstuffs had already been stored in Ark 4 but it took several weeks to load the livestock in Arks 1, 2 and 3. On the 40th day the water was deep enough to float the vessels. Noah had had the forethought to attach them in a long string by thick cables. Even with so much work to do the family paused long enough to gaze out in awe as the familiar landscape disappeared until not only the tree tops but even the tops of the hills disappeared.

The rest – essentially at least – is history, though God, as the winner, wrote it his way. Noah and his family who did all the work got minimal recognition. As the ultimate founders of the entire human race God thought their survival was reward enough. He had employed them to carry out his Grand Plan. He had destroyed the race which had defiled his creation by their thoughtless, selfish and downright evil behaviour. From now on, God believed, Noah's descendants would learn from this lesson and would care for the wonderful world he had created for them....

Temptation

There was no doubt, Jeremy had a chip on his shoulder. Born and brought up on a council estate, he viewed all wealthy, middle class people with contempt. How, he asked, could such people - and especially their offspring - justify their undoubtedly privileged lives? He had fought his way – literally at times – through primary school and the comprehensive. Afterwards he had contested job interviews with ex-public school boys, distinguished not only by their speech, but also by their carefully chosen, casual clothes, and the ease, verging on arrogance, with which they faced their inquisitors. He hated the way they made him feel inferior, although his rational mind told him he was at least their equal. By contrast, he had *earned* success and, at the age of 32, held a good post with the borough council. His sense of social justice was satisfied in such a public role.

He was unmarried. He enjoyed his freedom and engaged in casual relationships with a series of attractive young women. Sex was always consensual, enjoyed by both participants. Jeremy was a good-looking young man. He kept fit, working out at least twice a week in the gym, and he took pride in his appearance. Women found him attractive in their turn, something he understood and exploited. In these days of easily available contraception many of the old taboos had disappeared and Jeremy, for one, never for a moment saw such relationships as having any moral implications. He had learned a great deal about the art of seduction.

It was, thus, coincidentally that these two elements of his personality came into play one afternoon. He was on his way on foot to visit a council tenant. On his way he passed through an avenue lined with large houses behind well-tended lawns and shrubberies. As he walked, the usual thoughts ran through his head, contrasting the space and comfort enjoyed by the owners of these properties with the cramped, sometimes squalid flats on the estate. He was so preoccupied that he failed to hear the warning shout of the young boy on the scooter. The boy was very sorry, and Jeremy felt unable to be too angry, although the collision had torn his trousers and left him with mud on his sleeve and a gash on his shin.

An elegant woman in her mid-forties cane to his aid. She insisted on his coming into her house to clean up.

"You clearly need a dressing on that leg," she said. "I'm sure we can sponge the worst of the mud from your suit."

She spoke with the crisp, clean accent he detested. Her clothes were expensive in their simplicity, cut by an expert hand and suggesting a well-toned body beneath. She wore pearl earrings and discrete but flattering make-up. Her hair, expertly cut and tinted, was short, and her skin was flawless. She walked with the careless grace that comes with years of attention to deportment. Everything about her spoke of money and good taste.

Jeremy resolved there and then to expend the full force of his charm on her seduction. He responded to her small talk with careful flattery. When she took his jacket to sponge the sleeve, he pointed out that the stain had penetrated to his shirt. She fetched a bathrobe and told him to give her the shirt. Did he imagine it, or did her hand stroke his arm? And in handing him the bathrobe she really did not need to help him into it by also running her soft, well-groomed hands over his pectorals. To his startled amazement, she was seducing him! She took charge, washing the shirt, which would, she said, soon tumble dry. Meanwhile they might have a drink. She offered him a choice. He accepted a whisky. She took control of the conversation, asking questions about his work and making appreciative comments. She remarked on his physique, asked if he were married. He was out-manoeuvred.

By the time his shirt was ready Jeremy was also ready to succumb to her advances. To his surprise, however, when his cleaned and dried shirt was retrieved, she merely smiled indulgently.

"There," she said. "You look almost as handsome as before. You remind me so much of my son. He is young and splendidly fit like you. Will you be all right to walk home on that bad leg, or would you like me to drive you? My car's in the garage." She put the stress on the second syllable.

To his annoyance and embarrassment Jeremy found it difficult to reply without stammering.

"I'm fine, thank you," he said. "Thanks for your help."

As he left the driveway and turned onto the pavement he could feel her eyes on his back. He was confused to feel himself blushing, angry with himself, humiliated once more by someone who had proved a gracious but superior opponent in the class war.

The Bucket List

"What you doing?"

Henry looked up. The boy was probably eight or nine and he was watching the old man with open curiosity and candour.

"I'm writing."

"Writing what?"

"If you really want to know, I'm writing a bucket list."

"What?"

"A bucket list. Don't you know what a bucket list is?"

"No." The boy looked puzzled.

"It's a list of all the things you want to do before you kick the bucket."

"Kick the bucket?"

Henry laughed. "You don't know what kicking the bucket means? It means dying."

"You're not going to die, are you?" The boy looked alarmed.

Henry laughed again. "Not yet, I hope," he said. "Though I suppose I am getting a bit old. That's pretty obvious."

"I thought it was a bit rude to say so," the boy said.

Henry laughed again. "What's your name?" he asked. "I'm Henry."

"Brian."

"And how old are you?"

"Nine."

"Well, Brian, I'm nearly 9 times as old as you. How about that?"

Brian stared in disbelief. How could anyone be that old?

"I'll bet if you made a bucket list it would be very, very long."

"Haven't thought about it," Brian admitted. "So what's on your list?"

"Tell me what you put at the top of yours before I tell you what's on mine."

This made Brian frown in concentration, then he gave a little shrug. It was one of those impossible questions, the sort teacher might ask. How was he to know? "I don't know," he said, uncertain. "I suppose I'd like to meet famous people, people like the ones you see on telly, or...or footballers maybe."

"You like football"

"Yeah, don't you?"

"I quite like watching it these days but I don't think I'd be much good at it any more. What do you think?"

"What about when you were young?"

"Oh yes," Henry nodded, a slightly wistful look on his face, "I played quite a lot of games when I was young. I didn't look like this then."

"So go on," Brian urged him, "Your turn."

"My turn?" For a moment Henry did not understand. "Oh, my list! You'd probably find it quite dull. Right at the top I'd like to go back to America for a trip."

"You been there before?"

"Oh yes! Several times. My daughter still lives there."

"Wow!" Brian was impressed. "What's next on your list?"

"Well," said Henry, a slightly dreamlike expression on his face, "The first half-dozen items on my list are all trips to places I'd like to revisit that I used to know well. Number two on the list would be Zimbabwe."

"That's in Africa!" Brian was triumphant: he had heard of it. "We've learned a bit about that in school. You have been there?"

Henry laughed quietly. "I lived there for five years," he said. "I worked there for a bit."

"What were you doing?" Brian asked. "Farming?"

"Farming? No, I was a civil engineer." Seeing the look of incomprehension in the boy's face, he added, "I was building a bridge, quite a big bridge."

"My dad's a builder," Brian said. "He lives in Brixton. He comes to see me when he's not working."

Henry made no comment. He was thinking how sad that families so often seemed to break up. Brian was a likeable lad, full of curiosity, ready to learn, no doubt his prospects would be limited, one of so many children these days living in what was euphemistically called a single-parent family.

Brian was off on a new tack. "Do you live round here?" he asked.

Henry turned to point to the tower block at the far edge of the park. "Over there, in that block," he said.

"That's where I live!" Brian said, "We are on the fourth floor. Where are you?"

"Nearly at the top," Henry replied, "Floor 12."

"Do you like it that far up? Some people I know complain about being too high off the ground."

"Not me," said Henry. "I like the view. It's great, but I expect you know that."

"I told you, I live on the fourth floor."

"Now, Brian, don't tell me you've never bothered to take the lift up to the top to see what it was like."

Brian grinned. "Yeah, well, I'm not supposed to. Mum told me not to."

"Well, young man, next time you want to admire the view, tell your mum you have an invitation from me, tell her its Mr Bishop, flat 59. She can come and have a word with me herself if it makes her feel better."

. Brian's mother did, indeed, call on Henry, intending to give him a piece of her mind, suspecting he was "a dirty old man". Instead, she was charmed and she told Brian he could visit. It was a friendship which was to last five years.

At 14 Brian was a tall, athletic and intelligent teenager. Henry's adventures and travels continued to entertain him. He visited flat 59 two or three times most weeks. He was always polite. When he got no reply to his knock one Thursday morning, he waited a moment and then knocked again. Before he turned and headed for the lift he tried once more. This time the door of flat 60 opened and a lady spoke to him. "He's not there."

"I'll come back later," Brian said.

"You've not heard then," the woman said. "Mr Bishop is not coming back today or any other day. He passed away last night."

The lift was empty, the way his head felt. He pressed the button for the fourth floor. The doors slid open at last. As he turned towards his own front door he felt a constriction in his throat, tears began to run down his cheeks. It was so unfair, such a horrible shock. Henry had not crossed off a single item on his bucket list. One day, Brian said to himself, he would tick off those items in honour of his special friend.

The Corporation

When the buzzer sounded, the secretary flipped a switch and led the young man to the imposing double doors, high heels tapping. She opened one door for him. Even the entrance was designed to impress, as was the office. It was spacious, as befitted the President of this large corporation. It would normally have filled him with awe but he had been here before and anyway on this occasion his determination was such that he was almost unaware of his surroundings. It was fully 20 feet to the chair on his side of the desk. The desk itself was enormous and solid. On it sat an intercom system and three telephones in different colours as well as a wooden name plate with the President's name in gold letters. On the other side of the desk the President, a mountainous man with rimless glasses and a face of granite, showed no sign of welcome.

"Well? What is it that's so important?" The voice was belligerent. The young man, having reached the chair, its back and seat upholstered in leather, bearing the logo of the corporation, Q S C, stopped and made no attempt to sit down. Instead he met the President's gaze.

"It's the only way I can get to see you," he said. "Not many sons have to make an appointment to see their own father."

"You more than anyone must understand what

it takes to run a corporation of this size," his father said. "If you don't know now, you will certainly find out the hard way soon."

"I'm not going to do it," his son replied. His voice was steady, but a close observer would have seen the tension in his body and the absence of colour in his face.

"Not going to do what? Make yourself clear; don't talk in riddles."

"I'm not going to work in the Corporation." He had said it, that was the main point and it should make the second announcement easier.

"Not going to...?" The President rose to his feet. He was burly as a bear. He knew he looked imposing and he intended to be intimidating. "Of course you are going to work in the Corporation. I haven't wasted all that money sending you to the best schools in the country and paying for you to get a law degree at Harvard for you to waste it in some back street office working as an attorney." He gestured at the large portraits on the wall behind him. "This business was set up by your grandfather, Quint E Senschal the First. He named me Quint E Seneschal II, and you are Quint E Seneschal III. Of course you're going to join the Company. You'll get a hard training, but all this will be yours in time." He spread his arms wide to indicate the entire business.

"I don't think you heard me," his son replied, keeping his voice as steady and level as he could. "I'm not going to practise law: I'm going to be an actor.

I've joined a theatre company."

His father stared at him for perhaps a minute, open-mouthed, before his face was contorted in rage and his great fist crashed down on the desk with such force that the receivers jumped in their cradles. "By God! You will do as I say," he shouted.

Quint E Senechal III flinched but stood his ground. Now was the time for the *coup de grace*

"There's something else," he said. "Perhaps if you had been a normal father, had seen me grow up, it would have been clear to you already."

"What the hell are you talking about now?" The older man was still clearly furious. The second revelation, his son realised, might well be dismissed as sheer nonsense.

"I'm gay," he said. "I thought it best to tell you. And by the way," with a wide sweep of his arm he pointed round at all the oak panelling, the family portraits the certificates, the photographs of his father with statesmen and celebrities, "I know you will disinherit me, but I don't care at all. I don't want any of this. Oh, I am also changing my name. Lloyd Blanding." And with that he turned on his heel and strode all the way to the door without a backward glance.

Quint E Seneschal II watched the tall doors close on the end of a dynasty, then lowered his great body to sit heavily in his chair and stare, unseeing, across the empty room.

A part of the main

Emma scattered the last of the wheat for the chickens and dropped the bucket on the ground. 'I can't do this any more,' she said.

On the other side of the fence Joe straightened up in surprise.

'Not feeling too good?' he asked.

She didn't reply but stood motionless and looked at him.

'You didn't sleep well last night,' he said. 'You've been looking a bit off-colour.' He stepped over the wire . ' Sure you're not just tired? Why don't you go back to bed for once?'

With a flash of anger she retorted, 'Tired? I'm not just tired: I'm exhausted.'

Something in her voice stopped him in his tracks. Emma was aware of it herself. The well-modulated speech of the trained actress had given way to something more like the broken tone of a sick child. Words seemed to stick in her throat.

Joe came towards her, his concern plain to see, but she raised a hand weakly as though to ward him off. 'Don't,' she said, and he stopped, baffled.

She turned away and stared across the headland. The sea was restless, grey, reflecting the low cloud. Small, choppy waves rolled towards the shingle beach, unstoppable, relentless, never-ending. Two miles offshore a curtain of rain obscured the mainland. Behind her she was conscious of Joe, still not daring to move. She could feel his presence. In a gesture of despair she spread both hands as if praying to some elemental deity. As she did so she saw the roughened skin, the fine lines of ingrained dirt, the broken nails, once varnished and buffed. Then the tears came. She cried as though she would never stop, making no sound. The tears welled up and ran down her cheeks, dripped off her chin onto the grubby painter's smock she had brought with her together with the paints and brushes which remained untouched in their box.

Joe moved closer but took care not to touch her. 'Emma,' he began, but could find no way to break through this new, dreadful barrier between them. 'Emma,' he began again, but once more she raised a hand to one side to wave him away. Oh, my love, she thought, I'm about to break your heart.

At her feet the beady-eyed chickens continued to hunt greedily for every grain in the thin grass. She was aware that something had alarmed the geese, their honking loud but brief. A solitary gull paraglided on the updraught over the dark, wet cliffs. It was all so impersonal, she thought, so cold.

Her tears dried up at last. She turned to Joe but made no attempt to wipe her face. Yet again he tried to speak and yet again she put up a restraining hand. She had lain awake all night rehearsing this. In the warm, familiar bed she had gazed at his back, loving the way two years of daily hard labour had defined the muscles, left no spare fat. She had witnessed the good-looking, urbane lover become a strong, determined man, fulfilled and vigorous. Protective but not patronising, he shared his life with her, was grateful that she shared hers with him. In the last few weeks, Emma realised, doubt had seeped into her consciousness much as water seeps into rock until fine cracks become open fissures. She had rejoiced to see Joe so completely fulfilled, but it was no longer enough. She had recently for the first time experienced moments of regret, as when she saw herself in the mirror: she too had lost weight, was positively skinny, while her hair, exposed daily to rain and salt-laden wind, was uncared for and dull. Perhaps she had allowed her true interest to be suborned by his; her individuality has been merged, submerged.

When she spoke she was still not fully in control of her voice. 'I'm catching the ferry in the morning,' she said, not daring to meet his eyes.

It was as if they had been standing under a blocked gutter and her words released a gush of emotions. They both reeled under the deluge of dismay, disbelief, betrayal, guilt. Joe took an unsteady step backwards and groped for a fence-post for support. His shoulders slumped and involuntarily the muscles of his face relaxed, sagged, and his eyes seemed to sink. He had trouble breathing for a moment. Appalled, Emma's instinct was to run to him reassure him, comfort him like a child, but she could not. For the first time she felt she did not know what he was thinking.

'Will you be coming back?' His voice too was

different, half strangled.

Slowly she shook her head rather than answer aloud. Joe nodded that he understood. And all at once Emma experienced an extraordinary sensation as though she were back on stage and this was a scene in an angst-ridden drama. Even the gulls, wheeling against the grey clouds, the distant rumble of the shingle, the snuffling of the pigs in their pen, all seemed artificial, contrived effects.

There was nothing left to say, yet so much to say. They stood for some time until Joe turned and walked away. He moved like an old man. Emma picked up the empty bucket and went back to the croft.

Inside she began packing. The box of art materials went into the case first. She worked mechanically. Later she made tea, took a mug to Joe where he was working out of sight and sheltered from the wind. They could still find nothing to say, merely looked at one another in dumb misery. At dusk Joe came back and washed off the grime of a day's work at the kitchen sink. She had prepared a meal but neither of them could eat, and the food grew cold on the table. They sat either side of the turf fire. Its warmth gave them no comfort. Once more Emma began to weep silently, unable to stop, and this time it was Joe who reached out towards her with one hand which faltered and fell back, a hopeless, helpless gesture. Then to Emma's horror, he began to cry, great, racking sobs that convulsed his body as he acknowledged the death of his dreams.

They did not go to bed but fell asleep where they sat as exhaustion finally gave them a merciful escape for a few hours.

Joe took the old suitcase in his strong hands and carried it from the quad bike to the boat. On the jetty Emma turned to him. She had to say goodbye, but she did not know how. She had an unfamiliar, maternal urge to cradle him in her arms but knew she could not. Her whole body was tense, quivering with shock and fear. Overriding all other feelings was a sense of guilt. She embraced him for the last time and kissed him. It was like kissing a corpse.

She stepped aboard the ferry, wrapped her old, thick coat round herself and found a seat on the open deck. She knew Joe would remain on the quayside until the ship was out of sight. She pictured him like some ancient Greek hero, watching as she sailed off, each playing a part in a well-rehearsed, classical tragedy. Below her feet the heavy diesel engines throbbed. The ship's nose separated from the wharf and pointed towards the open sea, ready to meet the swell.

She did not look back.